First Green Line Edition, Crooked Cat Publishing Ltd. 2014

**FT
Pbk**

Discover us online:
www.crookedcatpublishing.com

Join us on facebook:
www.facebook.com/crookedcatpublishing

Tweet a photo of yourself holding
this book to **@crookedcatbooks**
and something nice will happen.

To my beta readers:
Juliet, Lucie and Jennifer.

The Author

Yvonne Marjot was born in England, grew up in New Zealand, and now lives on an island off the West Coast of Scotland. She has a Masters in Botany from Victoria University of Wellington, and a keen interest in the interface between the natural and human worlds. She has always made up stories and poems, and once won a crate of port in a poetry competition (New Zealand Listener, May 1996). In 2012 she won the Britwriters Award for poetry, and her first volume of poetry, The Knitted Curiosity Cabinet, was published in 2014 by Indigo Dreams Publishing.

She has worked in schools, libraries and university labs, has been a pre-school crèche worker and a farm labourer, cleaned penthouse apartments and worked as amanuensis to an eminent Botanist. She currently has a day job (in the local school) and teenage children, and would continue to write even if no-one read her work, because it's the only thing that keeps her sane. In her spare time she climbs hills, looks for rare moths and promises herself to do more in the garden.

You can follow her work via the Facebook group The Calgary Chessman, or on the Wordpress blog The Knitted Curiosity Cabinet.

Acknowledgements

Thank you to my fellow writer and poet, Juliet Antill, for always encouraging me, and for writing a timely and careful critique of the entire work at a very early stage, which gave me the impetus to carry on.

To my father, Michael, and my daughter, Ellie, who have always believed in me, even when I didn't believe in myself.

To Lucie and Jennifer, who have read the work at various stages and in various states, and have always been supportive and ready to produce cups of tea and shoulders to cry on when necessary.

To Tabby, my number one fan: an honorary Crooked Cat, if ever I knew one.

To my many friends on www.authonomy.com, who were never afraid to hand out tough love and harsh criticism when needed. Without you, it wouldn't be as good as it is.

To Jeff Gardiner, the kindest and nicest editor in the world. Be tougher, Jeff. I can take it!

To Crooked Cat, for doing me the honour of publishing my book, and to all my fellow Cats, for your support and kindness. I hope we will have a long and fruitful association.

Yvonne Marjot
August 2014

The Calgary
Chessman

Prologue

The darkness was absolute. Crouched on the top step, I clung to the smooth surface of the door. I feared falling: the basement stairwell yawned below me and without visual cues it was hard to balance. My hands on the door were the only reliable guide to my surroundings while my eyes persisted in trying to see something – anything. Closing them summoned up flashes of red and green, but when I opened them and peered into the darkness, I saw nothing at all. My ears strained constantly for his footsteps, coming back to complete the process of my humiliation. But mostly I feared he might not come back.

I swallowed down the rising dread that I might miss my boy's departure on his first day of school. Better not to think of that; allowing worst case scenarios into my head only made them more likely. He couldn't leave me here all night. Could he? I shifted a little on my uncomfortable perch, but a twinge of pain from my arm reminded me not to move. I closed my eyes again and willed myself to calm. Slowly the fear-filled darkness receded as I thought my way into a more pleasant memory.

I took myself far away, to a hot, yellow New Zealand beach where a small, sturdy boy clad in nothing but a sun-hat carried buckets of water to fill the moat of the castle we had just finished. I watched him as I decorated the towers with shells, stones and drapes of wet seaweed. Something which had started as a simple mound with a bucket-castle on top had spread to cover a vast area of ditches and piles, patted and shaped into turrets and bridges, tunnels and walls.

The little figure poured and trudged, filled and poured relentlessly, but still the water drained away before he could

3

return with the next bucket load. I knelt down beside him and wiped away the grubby tear-streaks. Then I set to work digging a trench, from the main moat towards the sea's edge. The task was hopeless: the receding tide gradually exposed more of the beach, and the sea slid further away. Sam gave in and passed his bucket to me, and hand-in-hand we wandered back to the picnic.

A few sandy sandwiches and a lukewarm drink later, Sam was successfully distracted: off this time in his shorts and beach shoes to investigate the rock pools. Considering the tears, I was reluctant to take him back when at last the tide began to turn. Sam insisted, though, and we climbed down the hill again at twilight, round the back of the farmhouse, skirting the old slip where bare rock was beginning to gleam in the growing dark. Down past the waterfall, with a final jump into my arms onto the beach, to watch the march of the tide against our battlements.

Sam was pleased to see the ocean finally rush up the trench and fill the moat but, to my amazement, he laughed with delight as the foamy wavelets, raised a little against an offshore breeze, made short work of his towers and walls. In a few moments, the whole construction had collapsed into a soggy pile, soon to be as flat as the beach around it.

I sighed, remembering other days when Sam and I had spent hours in the little cove, building and discovering – things about the world, and about each other. It sometimes seems as though all the other days of my life have been grey shadows, and only those golden Huna Cove days were truly lived. Almost all of my strong memories of Sam are focused there. Except for his birth, of course. I winced, and turned away from that. There are parts of my life I prefer not to think about. Embarrassing moments at school. Most of my marriage. And the events that began Sam's life, and changed mine forever.

My concentration wavered, and I opened my eyes again to darkness. I expected to feel the basement stairs and the enveloping dark, drawing me back into my nightmare, but something else was wrong. The ground beneath my body was bumpy and irregular, and my hand pressed against a rough, stone surface, not wood. I yelped as a cold sensation washed across my feet. That was water! I struggled to sit up, to draw my feet away, but I felt a rush of liquid soak my legs again as a terrible surge of pain swept upwards from my arm and across my chest. The red wave of agony washed across my mind and pulled me down into the darkness once more.

1

The wind was too cold. I was a fool to have come out without a coat: my calendar said it was spring, but no-one had told the wind off the sea. Sand stung my legs as I plodded down the beach, meandering just above the high tide line. Sparse grasses bound the sand around their roots, but much of the fine, white powder was loose, and the sea-breeze blew it around my feet. The sun was up, but thin and watery through a haze of cloud.

Calgary Bay is one of my favourite places. It nestles into the rocky shore of the north-western coast of Mull, no more than an hour's drive from the island's main town, Tobermory. The narrow, white crescent leaps into view as the winding road descends, the brightness of the sand enhanced by contrast with the steep slopes of weathered black and brown basalt surrounding the bay. Not many people live there and, although it's busy enough in the summer, there are times when for days on end I can find myself the only presence apart from the wind and the insistent voices of oystercatchers.

Fifty million years ago those black heights towered like the Himalayas above what would one day be Western Scotland, as the last remnants of the Tertiary igneous outpourings began to cool into features that we would tame with cosy names: Fingal's Cave, McCulloch's Tree. Now the basalt behemoths have worn down to battered nubs: the exposed roots of mountains, ground down by rain and frost and time. The landscape has become smaller, more human-scaled, softened by time and the changes we have wrought: fields green and smooth where the stones have been pulled out, walls of stone around pastures and houses, and the small graveyard with its poignant scatter of memorials.

I pushed my hands into my pockets and pulled my cardigan more tightly around myself, but the chill air crept in anyway. So much for a walk to blow away the cobwebs; it felt more as though they had been freeze-welded into place. I scuffed at the sand with my boots as I trudged up and down the half-mile crescent, noting as I glanced downward that the toes were wearing thin. That, and every small stone making its presence felt through the soles of my feet, reminded me that my boots were on their last legs. (Funny, Cas. Very funny. There's a certain freedom in being able to make really bad puns without being reminded that they're a low form of wit.) Anyway, I would definitely need a new pair before next winter. I love my slouchy, burgundy suede boots, perfect to slip on for a quick walk; a relic of a past life, when footwear was just another frivolous purchase. I couldn't imagine how replacing them was going to be possible.

I didn't want to think about that. I thought about the machair: a narrow border of grassland holding the sand together, a mosaic of tiny plants marking the boundary between the wild sea and the tamed farmland. A little patch of complex interactions, defining the space between control and chaos. Like me. Although the machair, at least, belonged here, and had done so for thousands of years. I was still trying to decide whether I did.

The sound of voices interrupted my reverie and I looked up to see a family of tourists making their way down to the beach. The mother, struggling with a beach umbrella, towels and a picnic hamper, gave constant advice to the two children about water safety, staying within view, and being careful. The man had already reached a flat spot in the dunes and was trying to set up a wind break. Well – they were going to need it. I met his eye as I passed, returned his friendly "Hello," and stopped for a moment to talk to them.

"Not the best weather for a trip to the beach."

"No, the wind's a bit cold. Might brighten up later though."

"Are you here on holiday?"

"Yes. We decided to take a week before the school holidays. Next year our boy starts school, so it's practically our last chance to get away early and beat the crowds."

We looked around. The turquoise waters of Calgary Bay lapped a wide and empty beach, completely bare of footprints. It was hard to imagine it could ever be crowded. He grinned at me and opened a deck chair for his wife who sank into it, replying politely to my small talk but distracted by the need to check on her children.

"Have you travelled far?" It was a silly question, really. They both had strong Midlands accents.

"Castle Vale, Birmingham."

"I don't know Castle Vale. It sounds nice. Is it a historical town?"

He grunted in amusement. "Tower block central, is what it is. Our two are lucky to see a building more than fifty years old from one year to the next."

His wife passed him a plastic cup of tea from a flask and he brandished it at me. "Care for a cup?"

"No, thanks, I'm fine."

He nodded and took a sip. The children, who had been hanging close by, were gradually becoming more confident. The girl was digging in the sand with a plastic spade and the boy had found a slope to climb.

"Are you here on holiday?" Close up, the mother still looked tired, but she had a sweet face. Her son looked like her.

"No, I live here. A few miles away, on the Dervaig road."

"You're lucky, to live in such a beautiful place."

"I know."

Having found their courage, the kids had ignored all their mother's advice. Possibly they hadn't heard a word of it. Now they'd both climbed to the top of the bank and were taking it in turns to roll down to the bottom, dislodging gobbets of sand as they went. I winced at the damage they were doing. The machair landscape of the Western Isles of Scotland is a fragile compromise between windblown sand, soil-binding plants and the power of the sea. Sheep and rabbits damage it and keep the plant cover thin, and it doesn't take much to break that cover and expose the sand to erosion. All it needs is a couple of kids rolling down a sandy bank.

I shrugged and moved on. People are only part of the problem – the sea does as much damage as all the visitors put together. This year, probably fuelled by the big westerly storm we'd weathered last week, the waves had reached right up to the edge of the machair and swept away a chunk of land, leaving the turf undercut. The work the sea does is not usually so obvious. Sometimes I can visit frequently over a period of months without noticing any change, but after a big storm there are always new scars.

I became aware that I was holding my breath. I told myself to relax, letting go the picture of Calgary scoured clean, all the white sand and the wildflowers gone back to the sea. The point of this visit was to walk away my worries, not to invent new ones. Thinking about my own concerns made me tighten my jaw again, unconsciously holding back between my teeth all the things that threaten to overwhelm me when I give myself time to think. (Let them go, Cas. Just breathe, breathe.) I fought down the urge to panic that seems to come over me so frequently these days. Things are not so bad, I told myself. It's all starting to come together.

Sometimes my mental to-do list seems overwhelming. In a few weeks time my beloved only son would be coming home for the holidays, and I didn't feel ready. Some of the worries were practical: the spare bedroom seemed to have become even damper in the last round of spring storms, and I'd had to swap over so Sam would have a dry, private space of his own.

I wondered about his ongoing relationship with his father, and about how he was getting on at school, but mostly I fretted about his behaviour. Last year he entered some kind of adolescent parallel universe where nothing made him happy, and even innocent remarks could trigger an outburst. Of course there were reasons for that, and some of them were my fault, although even so I didn't think they were adequate excuse for shouting, door slamming and sulking. The last time he'd visited, he'd been impossible to live with, and if this holiday turned out the same I didn't think I could cope. I had to, though. You only get one chance with your children. You have to make it work.

I quartered the beach, down to the water's edge and back to the machair, gradually becoming calmer as I wandered. I kept my head low, glancing out to sea occasionally when the waves came close, not focusing beyond the headland where haze on the horizon prevented me seeing even the closest islands. The greenish grey of the sea blended imperceptibly into the sky, and all the colours of the landscape were subdued. For a moment, I felt disorientated, as if gravity had inverted and I was walking upside down on a great curved dome, feeling that at any moment I might fall into the flat, featureless surface above me. I shook my head and kept my feet moving.

Slowly some memories seeped into my mind; images of a small boy flickered across my inner vision, like photos in an old album. It's easy to forget what treasures are tucked away in there, behind the grey divide. Sometimes they feel so immediate that they shock me right into that other world which was once so real. It's so much easier to live in the past than to face what is in front of me.

My foot scuffed against a tuft of grass and I came back to myself. I'd walked the beach up and down, and fetched up against the edge of the machair again. Last night's high tide and wind had dislodged a whole chunk of cliff edge, and the lump had slid down the dune-face, exposing a vertical slope of fresh, white sand. In it was a dark hollow, a deep space about the size of my fist. I put my hand in to see if it would fit. My knuckle grazed something hard. Scratchy. Not like the rounded pebbles and wave-smoothed pieces of driftwood lying on the beach.

I pulled my hand out quickly and shivered, thinking of sheep bones. Okay to look at, found scattered on the grass while out walking. Not so nice to touch, unseen. With a faint hiss, the little hollow collapsed and something rolled out of the hole and landed at my feet in a damp clump. I bent down to dig it out. My fingers closed on a pale ivory-coloured handful, a little darker than the sand, squat and squarish and about eight centimetres tall. Not a sheep bone. I pulled out my hanky, spat on it and rubbed the object. I stared at it.

I was holding something like a gnome sitting on a chair; rather ugly, but with complex, carved clothing and draperies. It was surprisingly heavy. The figure was vaguely familiar; even though at the same time I was sure I hadn't seen anything like it in my life. I went to drop it back where I'd found it, but changed my mind at the last moment and put it in my pocket. After all, I could easily throw it away later.

A superstitious voice in the back of my head muttered about omens. I'd come out today looking for something to knock me out of the self-destructive track of my life. Perhaps this was it? Or maybe it was more bad luck? Either way, picking up litter should make me feel good, and at least this was more interesting than the usual plastic bags and empty bottles.

I glanced back up the beach to where the family had set up camp. The boy was crying; I could hear his voice, piping like one of the little birds that run along the shoreline. He was in his father's arms, being comforted. The woman was down at the water's edge. She had rolled up her trousers to paddle, and the little girl jumped and splashed, clinging tightly to her mother's hand. The woman seemed happier, her stance relaxed. Was that because she was away from the man? Or were they the happy family they appeared to be? I wondered if I'd ever learn how to tell the good relationships from the bad, or whether perhaps all marriages were as secretly miserable as mine had turned out to be. Her husband walked over and she greeted him with a kiss and took the boy from his arms. She might have been smiling. I gave them the benefit of the doubt.

Folding my arms around my cold middle again, I lifted my head and tramped on. I wondered if I'd be able to persuade Sam to spend some time at the beach with me. It would do him good to come to a place where he could relax, with no demands placed on him. We spent a lot of time outside when he was younger, especially if his father was at home and objected to the noise and demands of a growing toddler. The beach was the best place of all. There Sam could run around and shout without anyone telling him he should sit down and be quiet, or that he was annoying or difficult or just in the way.

When he was wee, Sam had spend hours digging in the sand, creating shapes and structures that would otherwise exist only in his imagination. Even though he was a proper teenager these days, determined to be more grown-up than most adults, I was sure I could find something that would appeal to his underlying sense of fun, to drag him out of his rigid adolescent stubbornness, to make him show some enthusiasm. All I wanted was to find something I could persuade him to do together with me. How hard could that be?

Although, for all I knew he would turn up cheerful and calm, with the emotional storms of last year a distant memory, and I was wasting my time worrying about something that wasn't going to happen. I put part of my mind to puzzling out the labyrinthine complexities of a teenager's mind, and set another to dredging out the memory stirred by the strange little figure in my pocket. In the meantime, I licked the salt from my lips and turned my back on the wind, following a well-worn path across the machair to my car.

2

As I steered between the potholes, the loud honking of a horn drew my attention. I peered through the windscreen to see Bernie Kavanagh's old Volvo estate blocking the end of the track. She waved madly through her side window at me. I grinned, pulled on the hand brake and jumped out.

Bernie wound down her window and shouted to me. "Coming up for a brew?"

"Why not?"

She waved again and, winding up her window against the smoke belching from her exhaust, gunned the motor and pulled away. I watched her ancient vehicle making its way along the single-track road between the fields. I could feel the smile lingering on my face. Just seeing Bernie is enough to cheer me up. Nothing ever seems to get her down.

I got back into my car and followed her, keeping my distance from the evil smelling fumes. Bernie is an earth-mother extraordinaire: makes do, lives green and recycles everything. She says everyone is allowed one eco-crime, and her car is it.

As the vehicles wound their way round the headland and up onto the moor, the sun broke through a gap in the clouds and bathed a strip of the tussocky grassland in amber light. Paradoxically, the cloud ceiling seemed higher now I'd left the shore. Or perhaps the sun was finally going to burn through the haze? I slowed down, noting that Bernie's car had stopped a few hundred yards ahead. It jerked into movement again, and turned into a passing place. As it inched forward, I saw that it was taking evasive action to avoid a Highland cow and her calf, which were enjoying the warmth of the tarmac. They looked on phlegmatically, the cow chewing her cud, while I steered my small car neatly around the obstacle. Clearly, they weren't going to move for anything smaller than a fire engine.

When I pulled up alongside Bernie's house, she was lifting a small girl out of the rear seat. A gust of wind blew her blouse against her body and I made an interesting observation. Bernie was never one to beat about the bush, so I took a leaf from her book and attacked as soon as I opened my door.

"Are you pregnant again?"

Bernie made sure her daughter's shoes were firmly planted on the ground, then straightened and patted her tummy.

"Yep. To be honest, I thought I'd told you. Due in July."

I thought back. Did the news seem familiar? I had a horrible thought that maybe she had told me, and I'd forgotten. I felt a familiar misery rising – what use was I? How could I manage my own affairs, and look after a teenager, if I couldn't even be a good friend on the odd occasion when it was required of me? When Bernie turned to walk into the house I held back, feeling suddenly unwelcome, but I wasn't given the chance for self-pity. A small, warm hand inserted itself into mine, and Matilda tugged me towards the front door.

"Come on, Auntie Cas. We've got ginnerbed cats."

Bernie was banging things in the kitchen, coming out with two mismatched mugs, a plastic cup of juice and a plate of shapeless, pale brown blobs decorated with icing and chocolate buttons.

"Gingerbread cats," she said, to my quizzical look. "Tilly didn't want gingerbread men, and the only other cutter I had was a star. So Tilly made them herself."

"I'm sure they taste very nice," I said politely, taking one as Tilly jumped up and down next to the table, waiting her turn. Once her mother had taken her first sip of tea, with a sigh of pleasure as its steam wafted across the room, she grabbed two biscuits. Cramming one into her mouth, she picked up her cup and headed into the hall. Bernie watched her go, one hand idly rubbing the top of her tummy, and I leaned back in my chair, enjoying the warmth of my friend's company.

"Do you remember when Tilly was born?" she asked me. As if there was any chance I would forget. It had been a hot, humid August almost three years ago. As it turned out, it would be the last summer Drew and I would spend on Mull together. We'd gone down to the Salen Agricultural Fair. Drew went with Sam to look at the horses. I took refuge in the tea tent, where I was eking out a cup of tea and a scone, hoping to stay in my quiet corner until my men had immersed themselves sufficiently in things equine.

As I picked at the crumbs of my scone, I noticed a woman sitting alone at the next table. She was crying unobtrusively into her paper napkin, and from the way she leaned back from the table I could see she was heavily pregnant. I opened my mouth to ask if she was all right, when the pregnant stomach in question rippled in the unmistakeable movement of a contraction. She gasped and held her breath, gripping the table with white-knuckled hands. I slipped across from my chair to the one next to hers and laid one hand over her wrist. "Can I help?"

She shook her head. "My husband and son are out there." We both turned our heads to look through the flap of the marquee. A throng of people passed the opening, and filled the space outside. Over the hubbub of the crowd I could hear some kind of announcement, but the words were unintelligible from where we sat.

"Would you like me to try and find him?"

She shook her head again. "I think it's too late. Do you know the way to the medical tent?" She was already trying to stand. I stood with her, but as she pushed her chair out from the table, she groaned – a deep, protesting sound – and liquid gushed onto the floor. I suppose it wasn't more than a cupful or so, but it was so unexpected. At the time I'd nearly jumped out of my skin.

I grinned at Bernie across the kitchen table and laughed.

"Remember the expression on Mrs Maclean's face when your waters broke? I didn't know where to put myself."

Bernie giggled. "Think what it was like from my angle!"

I'd accompanied the woman, and a solicitous paramedic, across the ground to the medical tent, where we'd waited for an anxious hour or so of steadily increasing labour until her husband and son had finally been found. They escorted her to a waiting ambulance, which whisked her away to give birth to her daughter, but long before that happened Bernie and I had become firm friends.

I visited her and baby Matilda in the hospital, just before the end of our holiday. And when, last year, I finally stepped away from my marriage to Drew, and started to make a new life for myself here on Mull, it was natural to turn to the woman who'd become my friend when she was in need. Bernie was a good friend, and great company. Being with her always made me feel better.

I wondered, though, whether she thought our friendship was too one-sided. I didn't give much to the relationship. Here was Bernie, ready to dispense tea and sympathy whenever I needed it. She seldom asked anything in return. I watched her as she reached for the last gingerbread cookie. "What?" she said, scattering crumbs as she bit into it, "I'm eating for two. That reminds me. Are you around in July?"

"I expect so. Sam'll be here. He's coming for a visit at the end of June. I'm sure he won't cramp my style, though. What did you have in mind?"

"I'm planning a home birth this time. I'd like you to be there. Will you come, if I need you?"

My mouth hung open as I looked at her. I closed it and tried to pretend I wasn't astonished. "Are you sure? I mean, I'd love to be there. Just let me know and I'll come running."

"Thanks. It means a lot." Bernie swirled the cooling tea in her mug and ate the last chocolate button. "You won't be on your own. Jed will be there. Tom and Tilly too, in the early stages; then my Mum will come and take them away. The midwife will turn up at some point and take over, but I'd really like you to be there."

"Are you sure? I mean, it's such a private thing."

"Absolutely. Anyway, Jed's a bit of a fainter. You can stand ready to catch him and mop his fevered brow, while I get on with the job at hand."

That, too, was typical of Bernie. If there was one relationship I believed with all my heart was loving, mutually supportive and steady as a rock, it was Jed and Bernie's. I relied on the strength of their marriage to balance out the dreadfulness of my own. They're my proof that human interactions can be positive, even when times get tough. True, each of them made disparaging comments about the other – but there was no undercurrent of cruelty behind them. As far as I could tell, neither of them took any notice of the other's remarks. They were openly affectionate with one another, unafraid of what anyone else might think. I could learn a lot from them.

I drove down the hill with a smile still on my face. Bernie always kept me on my toes. She had a knack for dropping surprises into her conversation, but this one really took the cake. I wondered what I'd really be called upon to do, and whether I should make preparations, or just stand ready to drop everything when my friend called. At least this time she was planning to be home when it happened. I was almost home myself when I noticed the bulge in the pocket of my cardigan. I'd completely forgotten to show her the thing I'd found at Calgary Bay.

3

A big mug of tea steamed on the little table to my left, and next to it a pile of chocolate biscuits. I fantasised for a moment about real coffee (the nearest source being eleven miles away, in Tobermory) then picked up the mug, planted myself in front of the computer and logged on. As I waited for the screen to clear, I picked up the little figure from its place on the desk.

When I first arrived home with it, back in the spring, I cleaned off the sand and soil residue and stood it next to the computer monitor. It still looked familiar, but I couldn't place it. At first glance, I'd taken it for some kind of toy, but it was heavy and well made. It also had a presence. The expression the figure wore was severe: slightly supercilious but also, somehow, serene. I had the feeling my problems were far beneath its notice, so unimportant that they were not worth discussing. For some reason that was comforting.

I had carried on working, trying to make a house feel like a home, still missing my son and my old life, and hoping I'd soon start to feel at ease in my new one. Not for the first time, I reminded myself that starting a new life was going to require some kind of effort from me. I'd made feeble attempts over the winter to improve the house, and to find employment, but I was going to have to do a lot more to prove my independence. The thought was depressing and I allowed myself to be distracted by the figure I was turning around in my fingers, wondering if it was ever going to tell me its story.

A square base rose to become the back of a seat, geometric carvings merging with the intricate folds of the garment, part cloak and part skirt, which clothed the seated body. Stumpy arms protruded from the front of the cloak, and the figure rested its chin on one of its hands, staring broodingly forward. The presence of a crown gave a final confirmation of royalty, although the sumptuous throne and imperious expression would probably have been enough.

Almost sexless in appearance, clean-shaven and swathed in its cloak, it could have been of either gender. Something about it told me it was female, perhaps the queen of a vast, sandy kingdom, now captured to sit on my desk, brooding on the lost retinue of courtiers and servants of which I had deprived her. In truth, I was no nearer to working out what the figure was, or recalling whatever it reminded me of whenever I examined it.

Still, it was a pleasant handful, and I often found myself picking it up; stroking its carved and rippling patterns, or meeting the eye of the gnome-like figure. I did talk to it; sometimes it was the only thing I talked to in days. Once the week's shopping is done, I often don't see anyone for days on end. (Hobson's choice: talk to inanimate objects, or spend my time listening for the postie, so I can rush out to catch her for a few words of small talk.)

Anyway, it had begun to give sound advice, usually in the voice of my grandmother: friendly pearls of wisdom such as, "Bed now, or you won't want to get up in the morning," or "Brush your hair and put a skirt on. I don't know how you expect to get a boyfriend looking like that." Somehow, the passage of time had bred familiarity, and its remarks seemed less hurtful than when Nanna had said them. However, some of the more pithy comments were so reminiscent of my grandmother that I wouldn't have dared to answer back.

I set the figure down and reminded myself I was there to work. First, I opened the draft physics textbook I'd been proofreading and double-checked the last two chapters and the appendices. I'd only completed them late last night and wanted to be sure I hadn't missed anything. Then I began a letter to the editor:

'Dear Henry…'

Good old Henry. Far from taking sides in the dreaded divorce stakes, he had been as objective as a family friend could be. Most important of all, he had helped me to see that the Science degree I took through the Open University (one of the many time-wasting pursuits on which Drew resented me throwing away his hard-earned interest and dividends) could be of practical use. I was now gainfully employed as a freelance proofreader, primarily of scientific publications, and most of my work came from Henry. The combination of a fine eye for detail, a basic grounding in science, and the ability to meet deadlines had turned out to be a adequate income earner, and I was bringing in enough to feed and clothe myself (boots notwithstanding, though now it's a bit warmer I might need sandals instead) so long as I live fairly frugally.

At the moment, though, having Sam to stay will mean spending my savings. Not while he is at school, his father takes care of that, but when he comes for the holidays I have to find some way of paying for two of us to eat. I'm damned if I'm going to ask him to live off his allowance, although I'm quite sure that's what Drew intends. (Sorry, darling, Mummy can't afford dinner and the phone bill. Could you buy the food this week?) I needed to find another way of making money. But, for now, meeting the latest deadline should be the only thing on my mind. I stretched and yawned away my worries, then set myself back to the task in hand.

'Dear Henry,

Enclosed as required the proofs of the latest masterpiece. It reads well, if a little dry, but I suppose that is what's required. There's no problem with the text – I've annotated it in the usual way. However, you may like to take a look at figure 23c (Ch7, p232). The vertical scale there is given as micrometres per second, but in the adjacent text (p233) the scale is described in terms of millimetres. One or the other must be incorrect, or else the text seems not to relate clearly to the figure. I know this is outside my brief as your text proofer, so I hope you don't mind me mentioning it. Hope you and Marise are well. Have you met the boyfriend yet? Remember, if you ever need a change from the rat race, I have a spare room and all the peace and quiet you could wish for!

All my love,

Cassandra.'

I checked over the proofs one last time, made sure all was in order, and enfolded the lot, together with the letter, in a large bubble wrap envelope. After addressing it to Henry's publishing house, with my address on the back, I propped it in front of the screen. Resisting the urge to play a few rounds of mah-jongg pairs I closed down and walked away from the machine. With Sam due in tomorrow for the holidays, I wanted to finish the stencils on the kitchen wall before going to bed. The little figure peered from behind the envelope, scowled at my retreating back, and settled into its usual patient stance.

I worked for several hours on the stencils: sea-themed shapes in pale grey-green and butter yellow, on the creamy plasterwork I had finished sealing and painting a week before. Really, I can't afford to do much to the house until I sort out my imbalance of payments and income, but I wanted Sam to see I'd been doing something. The lobster shape looked a bit strange, but I was very pleased with the mermaid and the waving fronds of kelp. It felt good to be doing creative work again.

At last, when my fingers were too stiff to wield the brush accurately (worn down to the bone - better than bone-idle), I stood back and stretched. Too tired to judge anything properly, I washed the brushes and crawled off to bed. In the morning, I needed to get the parcel to the village shop before the once-daily post. I could walk round and still be back before Sam's bus arrived – I wanted to be there to see the look on his face when he saw the stencils. Silently, I prayed for a good start: let him find it fun. I can't bear it if he despises me. Please let it go well. Still pleading with the universe for something it couldn't provide, I fell into bed. Sleep came instantly, and no dreams.

With the morning, a cold wind blew in, and a few drops of

frigid rain. Halfway to the village, I regretted not getting the car out. Muttering about pneumonia and arthritis, I clutched the large envelope in its plastic bag and picked up speed. This ensured that I arrived at the shop glowing with heat, an effect which felt as embarrassing as it looked. ("It sets off your pale good looks," Drew said once. "Red-faced cow," it became later.) A couple of men were standing outside the pub, talking. An unrelated coincidence, I thought, since the pub doesn't open until lunchtime. They looked at me; I paid them no attention. Men do look at me. I don't know if they look at all women. I don't know what's normal, so mostly I pretend I haven't noticed.

The Post Office was busy, so no chance of a chat today. I posted the letter, paid for my milk and left, shoving the plastic bag into my pocket. Passing the village notice board, I spotted a new sign advertising the annual football match: 'Dervaig vs Salen, raffle to aid the village school, pig roast to follow'. It must have rained while I was in the Post Office, because the paper was damp and the colours were already beginning to run.

Walking home, I got into the lee of the hill, and after one vicious hail shower, the walk was quite pleasant. A bit of rainbow leapt into view over the loch, and as quickly disappeared as the next squall blew over. I ran for the house just as it arrived on my doorstep. After putting the milk away, I was on my way upstairs to turn down Sam's bed when I thought I heard the bus. I peered out the dormer window, but there wasn't anything on the road: either I'd been mistaken, or the bus had already gone past. I thought of hiding up here, jumping out at Sam when he came up, which would once have made him giggle. Too old now, too sensible (Sam, that is: I have no such illusions about myself).

Anyway, I hadn't heard the squeak of the gate; probably he wasn't even on that bus. He hadn't phoned to tell me which ferry he'd be on. Would he phone me? Drew never used to let me know: he would come home, or he wouldn't, whatever. He never did understand why I always wanted to know what he was doing all the time. (Get out of my head, Drew. Just go away.) I shrugged myself back into good humour and went downstairs again.

As I opened the door at the bottom of the stairs, Sam was there. He had his back to me, and I took a moment to check him over. He'd grown again: already as tall as me, I had a feeling he would eventually match his father's six foot even. He got his dark hair and pale skin from me, and his height and build from Drew, but as he spun round and grinned at me I was reminded that his grey eyes were all his own.

"I didn't know you were into chess," Sam said.

"Hello Sam. How are you? Was it a good trip?"

"Yes, Mum. But what about this?"

"That? I found it on the beach. I have no idea what it is. Why? Do you know?"

"It's one of the Lewis Chessmen. You know – we saw them in the first Harry Potter film. Wizard chess: this is the queen. In the film she picks up her throne and decapitates a bishop or something with it."

"Mmm…can't remember." I forbore to remind Sam that at the time he had been going through a patch of being embarrassed to be seen with his Mum. I'd taken him to the cinema, but he'd gone off on his own with his mates and I'd picked him up outside, afterwards. I had heard of the Lewis Chessmen, though.

"They were found in a sand dune on an island in the Outer Hebrides – Lewis, I suppose, since they're called the Lewis Chessmen. They're Viking, or something. But I didn't know what they looked like. Is that what you reckon it is?"

"Definitely," said Sam, who liked to be definite. "I wonder what one bit of a chess set was doing on a beach. You can buy them everywhere, you know. At least, everywhere that sells chess sets, that is."

I gazed at him fondly. It seemed the holiday was starting well

– at least we had managed not to start with hostilities. I racked my brain for further distractions, and then wondered whether he had even noticed the stencils. "Would you like a drink?" I asked, leading the way back to the kitchen. Sam set down the chess piece and followed.

"Fizz or juice?" I asked, leaning over the door. The fridge door has opened the wrong way from the day we first stayed here, but when we only came for occasional holidays it hardly seemed worth fussing. Now I'm so used to negotiating round it that I hardly register the irritation – except when I drop the milk in mid-lift and have a catastrophe to clean up.

"And what about lunch? I can do baked beans or scrambled eggs. Anything more complicated, and you can make it yourself!"

"Fizz, please, and beans," said Sam, looking round the kitchen. I almost missed his expression, as the expected cans hadn't met my searching fingers and I was forced to walk round the door and look into the fridge. I spotted two cans and handed one to Sam. He opened it and took a long swig. His eyes bulged. "What is this stuff?"

"I'm not sure," I said, defensively. "It was on special."

"It's awful. You drink it." And Sam handed over the pink can, in exchange for the unremarkable lemonade I was still holding. I sipped it cautiously.

"I hate to agree with your taste in anything," I remarked, "but you're right about this stuff. It is terrible."

"Typical of what middle-aged, middle-class mums drink, I would have thought," challenged Sam. He ducked as I swiped at him with the wooden spoon. "And speaking of middle-class pursuits, I do like your stencils. The fairies are a bit funny looking, but I like the dragons: they're really effective."

"That's mermaids and lobsters, you ignorant lout," I growled in mock outrage. Sam laughed and fled the kitchen, aiming his empty can in the vague direction of the bin as he ran. I could hear his giggles receding in the direction of the staircase.

"And take your case with you," I shouted, as I groped in the drawer for the tin opener. "Cheek." I gazed out the window and stirred the beans aimlessly round the pot as another spatter of hailstones hit the window, a small but satisfied smile lingering on my face. It had got off to a good start after all.

4

It didn't last long. Late the next morning Sam sloped downstairs, dressed but unkempt, and slouched into the kitchen. He clattered about, complaining that there was nothing to eat. He didn't like the available cereals. I'd stocked up specially, with the two he'd chosen for himself in the Co-op last Christmas. He wanted coffee. I found a half-full jar of instant down the back of the cupboard but it was a congealed mass, adding insult to injury. He didn't want toast, or eggs, or…and so it went on. He threw himself onto the sofa with a jam sandwich and scowled in my direction. I tried to look noncommittal, not sure what effect any facial expression might have.

"Have you any plans for the holiday?" I asked quietly.

Sam replied with a grunt. Then he roused himself. "There's nothing to do on this god-forsaken island," he snarled. "What's the point of asking me what I want to do, if there's nothing to do?"

I recognised the rhetorical question which would open the floodgates to disaster if I tried to answer it directly. I've been in this place before with Sam, when life isn't going exactly as he expects and he loses his temper over something he cannot control. (Rather like his father, I thought, refusing to admit that there was any resemblance to me in his behaviour.) I tried a flanking manoeuvre: sometimes, if I can get Sam onto a particular grievance, it clears the air of all the non-specific ones that are swimming round in the ether waiting to crystallize into excuses for outbursts of frustrated rage.

"Do you have any school projects to work on while you're here?"

That did the trick. Sam went off into a tirade about the misery of being stuck in this hovel with just his mother (in tones of vitriol) for company, and all she can think to do is to banish him to his room to get on with some 'school project'. He knew I was doing it to get him out of my hair. I just wanted to get rid of him and he'd only been there five minutes. He was damned if he was going to knuckle down to schoolwork when he'd hardly had time to catch his breath. (I caught *my* breath – I can hear myself saying the exact same phrase to my grandparents when they wanted help round the farm in the holidays, and all I could think was that I had just escaped the endless round of exams and wanted to fall in a little heap on the sofa with a packet of biscuits and half-a-dozen new books.) He needed a holiday first. "In fact," Sam scrambled to his feet, "I'm going to ring Ewan right now."

"Ewan?" I was astonished.

"Isn't that what I said? He told me at Christmas that if I was here in the summer he'd take me fishing. I'm going to ring him right now. Is that a problem?"

"No," I said. I remembered Sam and Ewan in deep conversation after Christmas dinner. Ewan and his Dad had been going to spend Christmas on their own, and Sam and I were going through a not-really-speaking-to-each-other phase: beginning to get used to the new situation, and the strangeness of being in the family's summer house during the winter, and heaven only knows what else was rattling Sam's cage at the time. It had seemed like a nice idea to have some company, and perhaps a distraction for both of us.

The day had been pleasant, apart from Sam's mumbled conviction that Ewan and I must be having an affair – why else would I bother to cook for him? This was such a Drew remark that I let it slide right over my head without comment. There's no defining the relationship I have with Ewan, except to state baldly that we are not lovers, and I don't feel it appropriate to discuss it with my son anyway. I'm entitled to have friends, and

Sam is obliged to be polite to them. End of story.

I hadn't registered, though, that Sam had been forging a friendship of his own with Ewan. That might be a healthy sign. Anyway, a fishing trip would get him out of the house and involved in something tangible, which could be all he needed to move on from post-school ennui to constructive use of his holiday time. In the background, Sam was phoning Ewan. I could hear his low voice, but it didn't sound like a conversation. Sam slammed down the receiver (I opened my mouth to comment but thought better of it) and walked back into the living room. "He's away with the boat. I left a message. It didn't say when he'd be back."

"Why don't you pop round to his Dad's? I'm sure Molly needs a walk."

Ewan's Dad, Hector MacInnes, had an old and much loved retriever bitch, but the old man was no longer able to get out and walk her every day. Usually Ewan walked her (or ran her, as often) and sometimes I joined him for part of the run. But when Ewan was fishing, or on a long tourist trip, Hector and his dog were left on their own. Sam jumped to his feet, startling me, as I hadn't expected such an enthusiastic response to my suggestion. He strode over to the window and thumped the pane.

"Look at that, Mum," he shouted. "Does it look like dog-walking weather?"

Outside the sky had blackened and sheets of water were running down the pane. As I looked, I heard the sudden drum roll of hailstones on the path, and the room darkened another shade. Thunder rumbled and a distant glimmer illuminated, just for a moment, the drops of water clinging to the glass. Sam leaned gloomily on the windowsill and tried to peer at the shrouded garden. "It's like being underwater," he said. "You'd drown if you went out there."

I agreed. It seemed best. Sam wandered about the room aimlessly, his fit of anger gone as quickly as it had arisen. He picked up the chess piece and perched on the edge of the desk as he examined it. He turned it in his hand, first gazing at the rain-covered window, then turning his attention to the figure itself. He began to examine it more attentively, and ran his fingers over the folds of drapery and the pattern carved on its back. He held it close to his eyes and squinted slightly.

"You know, Mum," he said, "I don't think this is a copy of the Lewis Chessmen."

"Well," I said, unable to resist teasing, "it can only be a copy of one of them."

"No, Mum. You're not paying attention."

I sat up straighter and shut my mouth. (Don't laugh, Cas, just don't! Was that a genuine bit of Sam's personality coming out, or an unconscious imitation of the didactic style of one of his tutors?)

"It looks like the white queen from the Lewis chess set. But in the cracks of our one there are bits of red, as if it was painted, and the paint has rubbed off. It's really heavy. It's damaged, too – look."

I obediently rose and came to look at the little figure. Sam showed me that its edges were worn and knocked about, and there was a thin crack running through the base. Now Sam had pointed it out, I could see traces of red pigment deep in the folds of the robe and the patterned carving of the throne.

"That rubbing and cracking could come from it being in the sea," I argued. "It might have floated in from somewhere, on the high spring tides. Although my first thought was that some child had buried it."

"I don't think so. I think it might be real."

"What do you mean, real?"

"I mean, really real. It might be one of the real Lewis chessmen. Maybe it's been floating around in the sea for hundreds of years and has finally ended up on Mull. It could be a real Viking treasure."

I eyed the piece again. "Not hundreds of years," I said. "It would be eroded away to a nub of rock by now. Or a nub of whatever it's made from, anyway."

Sam looked downcast.

"But it could be real," I added hastily. "I suppose it could have been washed out more recently, and come ashore just before I found it. The tides were especially high this spring."

Sam was excited again. "Maybe there's a burial site at Calgary Bay. Let's go there now and you can show me where you found it."

We turned to look out the window again. The hailstorm had passed and a steady, soaking rain was sheeting down into the garden. We looked at each other. Sam grinned. "You're still an incomer, Mum," he laughed. "I bet the locals get on with it despite the weather."

He was right. Fishing, farming and forestry go on every day, regardless. Whether it's tree-planting, lambing, salmon-farming or showing the tourists around in the hopes of sighting an eagle, life carries on. I had been known to pull on my oilskins and head out into a storm, if I had a postal deadline to meet or I'd run out of food. However, I wouldn't get soaked by choice, and I recognised that working in the dry was one of the advantages of a desk job (or home computer job, as the case may be).

"Townie, yourself," I muttered affectionately, and ruffled Sam's hair.

"Don't touch the hair," he said automatically.

"All right, then. How could we find out about this 'real' archaeological relic without getting wet?"

"British Museum," said Sam immediately.

"Silly," I said. "That's in London. We can hardly pop down for a look in their display cases. It's hundreds of miles away."

It was Sam's turn to look indulgent. He rose from his perch and patted me on the head. "Haven't you heard of the internet?" he said. "All you need to do is search for their website. You're part of the island whatsit-thing with all the

31

computers, aren't you?"

"Yes." If it hadn't been for the Digital Communities Project, which supplied every household on the island with a free computer and a year's internet access, I wouldn't have been able to work for Henry. The package had been a lifesaver, and I used it to exchange occasional e-mails with Sam during term time. As for really making use of the internet, though, I was much more wary. I worried I might get onto some unpleasant website by accident or catch a virus that crashed my computer. That would be my whole income, my livelihood down the drain. Of course I had an anti-virus package, but it doesn't do to take unnecessary risks.

"Look, Mum, I'll show you. What's your password?" Sam was already logging on. He caught my eye and grinned. "You can trust me, Mum, and I promise I won't do anything risky."

I was glad I'd had the foresight to create a separate account for Sam, which gave him access to most functions but protected any confidential material I might get from Henry. Ironically, the picture I'd chosen for his user profile was a chess piece. I made him turn away while I logged in, but he was back at my shoulder when I opened the browser and started scanning the text boxes and pop-up ads that filled the screen. Sam was in his element. He leaned over my shoulder and appropriated the mouse. A few seconds later, he was onto the British Museum website. It was that easy.

In fact, it was easier than even Sam had anticipated. It turned out the British Museum had recently produced an exhibit about its 'Top Ten Treasures'. There had even been a TV programme about them, and one of the ten treasures was: 'The Lewis Chessmen'. There was even a suggestion they might return to Scotland on loan, to be displayed in their home country. Sam downloaded the information and we began to read.

5

Silence reigned for some time. Rain crawled down the windows in rivulets, which slowed to a trickle as a wind arose and tossed the trees about. Everything was dripping and clean: the air free of dust, the sheep white, and the grass gleaming with raindrops. At last, the rain stopped altogether and a thin sunlight crept out, making the garden steam. Sam and I read on, oblivious, until a finger of sun sneaked in and reflected off the computer screen.

"Well, they weren't Viking, anyway."

"What have you found out, Sam?"

"It says here that the Lewis chessmen were found at Uig on the north-western coast of the Isle of Lewis. They were dated to about 1150-1200AD. I studied the Vikings for my special history project last year." (And in primary school. I well remember 'Samfast the Extraordinary' and his large cardboard axe, who struck fear from behind the kitchen door for a whole summer holiday in year 5. That was a precious insight into his school life.)

"They started raiding at the beginning of the ninth century, at the same time that the Book of Kells was being made in Iona. The abbey on Iona was abandoned in 850AD – because of the raids – so they must have been around Mull a lot at that time. But in the end the Scots defeated the Vikings and the raids stopped."

"That must have taken a long time because the Battle of Largs didn't happen until much later," I said. "Yes, it says here 1263. Scots versus Norwegians. It doesn't say Vikings though. I wonder when they stopped being called Vikings. The trouble is that it's really hard to tell the difference between Vikings raiding and going away again, settlers coming in and taking land for themselves, and Scandinavian rulers wanting to control the whole of Western Scotland. They even seem to have fought among themselves. But eventually things settled down, with kings and chieftains coming to agreements, rather than independent shiploads of warriors invading indiscriminately and taking what they wanted. I think the change had as much to do with events in Scandinavia as with the Scots fighting back. After that there were still lots of Norsemen around, but they were traders and settlers, not raiders."

"So the Lewis chessmen were too late to be Viking. Why did you think they were in the first place?"

"I thought I had read something about them," I mused. "Ah, here it is. 'They were probably made in Norway, and brought to Lewis to be traded'. I suppose in my foolish youth I thought that Norway and Vikings meant the same thing."

"Mum, you probably knew the Vikings in your foolish youth."

"I'm not as old as all that, you cheeky hound. Now, what else have you found out?"

Sam shuffled his pile of printouts. "It wasn't just one chess set that was found. It says here there are ninety-three chessmen, some in the British Museum, and some in the National Museum of Scotland, in Edinburgh. Some of the pieces are much bigger than the others, too. That's another reason they think there were several sets. They were all found in a cache under the sand at Uig. There's a picture here, Mum." He held it out. It showed a number of the pieces found on Lewis, including a seated figure very like ours. "That one's a queen; the one with her head in her hand and a fed-up expression. But our queen is fiercer – she looks as though she's in a right mood!"

"So would you be, if all your knights and soldiers had gone off and left you unprotected. Queens have their dignity, you know."

Sam picked up the little queen and looked it in the eyes.

"Don't worry, Ma'am, I'll protect you." He grimaced wickedly, trying to look fierce.

"Sam, do you remember Samfast the Extraordinary?"

"Oh, shut up, Mum."

I was still intrigued by the picture. "I can see a king – bit feeble looking, although he is holding a sword – a bishop and some knights and pawns, just like a modern chess set, but who is this guy with the teeth?" I pointed to a standing figure, holding a shield. Like the knights, he had a conical hat and held a sword, but his eyes bulged and a huge set of buckteeth protruded over the top of the shield.

"That's a warder, Mum. It's a kind of rook. That one's a berserker." Sam struck a pose and declaimed something I vaguely remembered from his school project. "They were the most fearsome of Norse warriors, and would work themselves into a red rage of bloodlust before a battle, so that they would feel neither pain nor fear, and wouldn't stop until they or their enemies were completely destroyed. They bit their shields as a sign they were ready for anything."

"I can see why that would appeal to you," I said. "Was there any less bloodthirsty information in this special project of yours?"

"Well, even in the times of heavy raiding not all Norsemen were Vikings. Viking just meant the raiding parties, and the same people could be farmers or traders at another time of the year. A bit like football hooligans being bank clerks on their days off."

"Very funny. Go on."

"The Norsemen who raided and traded with Scotland came mostly from Norway, and apart from the fishing there wasn't a great wealth of natural resources there. No precious stones or coalmines; no great tracts of arable land; harsh winters and short summers, and not much else to make life pleasant. They raided for treasure, and for slaves to trade in the markets of Europe. A lot of so-called Vikings went off into Europe and

Russia to work as mercenary soldiers. The Emperor of Constantinople had a Norse bodyguard called the Varangian Guard. Norse traders settled in Russia, and some of the people in that area are descended from them.

"They invaded Lewis in the middle of the ninth century, and other parts of Western Scotland, especially the islands. That's why so many Gaelic words come from Norse, especially place names. It's been shown that many people in the Western Isles and the Hebrides and Ireland and the Isle of Man are of Norwegian descent."

"I've got a snippet for you, then," I said. "The Normans who invaded England in 1066, and forced the Scots to make peace a few years later, were descended from Norse mercenaries who had carved out a kingdom on the edge of France. When the researchers who discovered your Norwegian descendants in Scotland came to southern Britain, they couldn't distinguish between descendants of Norse settlers, and descendants of the later Normans, because they were all kin."

"I remember that. We must have seen the same programme. I thought you didn't get TV?"

"This was on ages ago. Before we moved."

"Oh." Sam dropped the topic immediately. 'Before we moved' was associated with unpleasant memories, and the idea of discussing it was uncharted territory. Sooner or later we were going to have to talk about Drew, and about the divorce. Up till now there had never been a good time to do it, and it wasn't going to happen today. Our new found comradery was a pleasure, especially considering the behaviour I'd expected, and I certainly wasn't going to do anything to break the mood. I forbore to comment further and Sam steered away into safer waters.

"What about these chessmen, then?"

"I've been thinking about that," I said. "The Lewis Chessmen are dated to about the middle of the twelfth century, aren't they? By that time, the Normans had subdued Britain, the Lord of the Isles had been established here in the Hebrides, and the Middle Ages were well under way. Some people were quite prosperous, and there would have been lots of trading for luxuries.

"Places like the Outer Isles weren't isolated then, because most trading was done by sea. So islands were good landing places and trading posts, and were the centres of merchandising, especially in Scotland, where the mainland terrain was so harsh. It says here that by the end of the eleventh century chess had become a popular game among the aristocracy of Europe. So it wouldn't be surprising if a Norse trader or craftsman was travelling around the Western Isles hocking off the kind of luxury goods every wealthy household wanted to display."

"Why do they think it was a trader who buried all those chess pieces?"

"They're all made of walrus ivory or whalebone and nearly all the pieces found were major pieces. There are enough similarities to suggest they may have all been made by the same person. There were hardly any pawns, but there were some 'blanks' of unused ivory. Maybe they were being traded by the guy who actually made them. He would get his customer to pick the major pieces he liked, and then carve up a few pawns on the spot to complete the set. It seems that for whatever reasons, he cached his whole stock and never came back to collect them."

"Do you reckon the same guy made our queen?"

"There's no reason to think so. She looks a bit like the Lewis queen in your picture, but only superficially. For all we know, it was the convention for the queens to be seated on thrones with grumpy expressions. They are the most powerful piece on the board. There could have been more than one person trading in ivory pieces in the Hebrides. We don't know yet if our lady is from the same time as the Lewis Chessmen."

"Come off it, Mum. The Lewis queens are all sitting down with their heads on their hands, and so is ours. Some of the

Lewis pieces were stained red, and ours has traces of red pigment in the cracks. It looks as though it might be made from ivory – I think it's a bit smooth to be bone. Ours can't have been in the sea very long. It says here they are very susceptible to cracking if they get very wet or dry, because they absorb water easily. There's only a small crack in the base of our one. So it must have come from somewhere very close to Calgary Bay, or maybe even from the sand dunes themselves. Maybe there's another ninety-two pieces out there waiting for us!"

"I must admit, the similarities are remarkable," I said. "I think we ought to contact whoever is the right authority in these cases. I'm not sure where to start. It hardly seems like a police matter."

"Mum," said Sam, impatiently. "Don't you remember Ewan telling us that if we needed to find out anything, Sergeant Morrison was the person to ask? Ewan says there are only two policemen on the island, and they know everybody and everything."

"A slight exaggeration," I said. "I believe he told us there were only two police officers in Tobermory. But they still cover a huge tract of ground, and you're right: they are the people to ask. They'll know what we should do."

6

The next morning saw the two of us board the ferry for Oban, heading for an 11 a.m. appointment with Mr Niall Webster of AIAS, Argyll and the Isles Archaeological Survey. I hoped he wasn't the same person I had spoken to on the phone yesterday – a difficult call with a rude and abrupt man, who had made it clear we were probably wasting his time. I was convinced we were. I'd lost all confidence in the case Sam and I had built up. More than anything, I feared making a fool of myself.

Sam, however, was cheerfully optimistic. He remained enthusiastic about our discovery, pointing out that even if it was from the Middle Ages, figures like the warder-berserker led straight back to a Viking heritage, probably made for wealthy medieval merchants whose ancestors hadn't been raiding for generations. He was clearly looking forward to meeting a real archaeologist. Sam seemed to have only one image in mind for such a person – bearded, scruffy, beer-drinking and male.

I smiled to myself, remembering previous enthusiasms, and refrained from raising the issue of female role models. Over the years I'd weathered many of Sam's sudden passions for unusual and interesting occupations, and this looked like being the latest. It could be worse: last year he had been planning to fly space shuttles for NASA. It's hard to imagine a more unlikely career for a schoolboy from New Zealand, or Scotland for that matter. I didn't deal with that one very well. I told him he was being utterly unrealistic, and should consider more attainable careers. After all, what was the chance of him ever even visiting the shuttle base, let alone achieving a career as an astronaut? Especially with the final shuttle launch scheduled in a few weeks' time.

It was quite sad to reflect that I'd been born during the era of space exploration and the end of it could potentially come during my lifetime. I'd been forced to eat my words last year though, when Sam produced a newspaper article about a group of Scottish schoolchildren who had been hosted by NASA, and a printout of information about Space School.

I'll admit he caught me on the hop, and I had to apologise, but he's never really forgiven me for not believing him, or believing in him. He's right, too. I could have just supported him, and given him time to work out whether it was the right direction for him. He was only fifteen, with everything ahead of him, and I was wrong to try and limit him before he'd even begun his working life. I can still remember the humiliation at age ten when I stood up in front of a class of wannabe nurses and air stewardesses and told them I wanted to be an Egyptologist. Even the teacher laughed.

How little effort it would take to approve a child's choices, knowing they will change and change again as they grow and learn. (After all, here I am, dabbling in archaeology for real. Will that childhood humiliation come back to haunt me when they tell us we've been carting around a plastic replica? Just as well we're on the ferry, or I might be tempted to turn around and go home. Courage, Cas.)

The little chess queen was safely wrapped up in a tea towel in the bottom of my handbag. I hated carrying the thing – I much prefer a backpack, or big pockets, but I had decided to bolster my confidence with a smart skirt and jacket, so a handbag it had to be. At least it had a shoulder strap, allowing me to keep my hands free. I wore neat, low heels too, but my feet hurt already. I don't wear them often enough anymore. It's all bare feet round the house and wellies in the garden.

Drew used to hate me walking around the house in bare feet. If I did it in his home he would walk very close to me and then deliberately stand on my insteps, to remind me of his disapproval ("I'm not going to waste words on you"). I shuffled from foot to foot and eased one heel out of its shoe for a moment while I leaned on the railing and gazed out to sea. The surprisingly cold wind ruffled my hair and I pulled back slightly from the rail.

Summer's a good time of year to see dolphins and porpoises in the Sound of Mull, and they seem to like riding the ferry's wake or bow wave, but I couldn't see any today. I shrugged the bag back onto my shoulder for about the twentieth time and turned to Sam. He was gazing enraptured over the side of the ferry, leaning out so far that I nearly grabbed him. I swallowed the impulse because I knew that to give in to it would embarrass him completely.

The ferry was passing the narrow neck of the sound between Duart Head and the Lismore lighthouse. It's a treacherous stretch of water and often, as the ferry passed through, I'd seen fishing boats or yachts waiting well away from the swirling currents until the ferry's wake had passed, then making the journey a circumspect distance behind. Sam had spotted something much more exciting than a fishing boat.

A pair of otters was swimming abreast of the ferry. Perhaps they had been fishing in these turbulent waters and been caught out by the ferry's speed? Or maybe there was some advantage to them in venturing so close to the boat's wake? They were clearly otters – too small for seals, and they had an altogether different way of swimming: lithe and swift, the sinuous movement of their backs clear as they jaunted away from the boat, surfing on the wake. I saw the long tail of one as it curved over and dived, reappearing a few feet closer to the lighthouse.

I breathed a sigh of sheer delight. It's always an unexpected pleasure to see an otter, and it's impossible not to feel your spirits lift as you watch the playful way they pursue their lives. I'd never seen anything like this before. I was feeling better already: even a disastrous meeting with Mr N.W. couldn't spoil the day now. Sam's eyes were shining as he turned towards me, delight written all over his face. There's that wonderful grin I love so much. A few years ago it would have been the immediate prelude to a hug, but today I was pleased enough to get a spontaneous show of happiness from my moody adolescent. I was surprised the sun hadn't come out in response.

Half an hour later we were not so happy, as we slogged uphill in the rain towards the address of the AIAS offices. Sam moaned continually about how wet he was, how cold he felt and how little he was looking forward to dripping all over some stranger's floor. Privately I agreed with him, but I ignored the diatribe. I'd decided not to bother with a taxi, as it takes no longer to walk straight up to the higher streets of Oban than to go the long way round the one-way system in a car. However, I hadn't banked on the sodding (ha, bloody ha) great grey cloud that had blown across the bay and dropped its contents all over us.

By the time we had found the right address we were soaked through and Sam had finally shut up. A quick glance at his face confirmed this was not because he had accepted the situation. He glowered blackly at me and pointedly turned away. This did not bode well. I hoped he would keep his temper with this Mr Webster, especially if he turned out to be the rude man I had spoken to over the phone.

He was. I recognised the voice, and the manner, as he reluctantly invited us in. We dripped, as Sam had feared, all over the lobby, and even when we had been shown where to hang our coats we thoroughly dampened the chairs in which Mr Webster invited us to sit. I looked him over: a youngish man, perhaps in his late twenties, of moderate height, wearing a nondescript jacket over dark shirt and trousers, albeit well-made and beautifully cut.

He was just as surly as he had seemed over the phone, but I was hardly aware of all that: I was captivated. He was simply the most beautiful looking man I had ever met. He had broad shoulders tapering to a slim waist and hips, eyes an amazing shade of green, skin so perfect it looked as though it was airbrushed, hair lightly tousled, streaked in shades of blond. (Too perfect. Is that hair dyed? Is he really too good to be true?)

I blinked and cleared my throat nervously. I had no idea what he'd said.

"Mrs Longmore, do you have the object?"

"Oh…yes. Of course." I began explaining how I'd found the chess piece, at the same time rummaging through my handbag, which as usual seemed to be full of half-used packs of paper hankies and packets of boiled sweets I didn't remember buying.

"Please don't tell me anything yet. Show me the object, and I'll tell you whether we are all wasting our time."

I unearthed it and handed it over. He unwrapped it with great care; an act which endeared him to me, since it was clear he did not expect it to be of any interest whatever. He hefted it in one hand and lifted it to his eye level. His face froze. Without taking his eyes from the little queen, he reached beside him to his desk and picked up a hand lens. Scrutinizing the figure with great care, he turned and began to make notes, at one point exchanging the hand lens for a larger one that attached to his head with an elastic band and pulled down over his forehead. The magnification must have been really powerful, because I could see those emerald eyes larger than ever, fixed securely on what he was holding.

I glanced at Sam and, at the same moment, he turned and looked at me, then grinned through his soggy fringe. We turned back to Niall Webster. He seemed completely unaware that we were still in the room.

After several minutes, he set down his pen and sighed, then he turned to us with a small movement of surprise. I was right – he had totally forgotten our presence. For a moment he seemed lost for words, and when he did speak his manner had completely changed.

"I believe you may have found an object of real interest. This certainly appears to be of genuine antiquity, and I will need you give me as much detail as possible about the location and manner of its finding. Let's have some coffee before we begin: this will take some time."

Mr Webster ("Call me Niall") was as good as his word. After providing us with large mugs of (proper!) coffee, liberally sweetened in Sam's case, he drilled us without mercy for two hours. He made me describe the finding of the chess queen, going over the details again and again. He talked through with us the geology of the beach at Calgary and its surroundings, and asked me again to review the scene and try to be more specific about the area where I had found the piece.

He brought out map after map of the area, each one larger in scale, ending up by pulling out a huge hand-made map of northern Mull, scribbled all over with symbols and unintelligible handwriting. I could see marks at the sites of the standing stones at Dervaig, and the abandoned village at Crakaig, and guessed this was Niall's own map of archaeological sites in north Mull. There was nothing marked over Calgary beach itself, but x marked the spot of each house site in the little village of Inivea, on the hill above the bay.

Niall folded the map carefully, so that Calgary became the focal point, with most of the written information hidden from our eyes. I couldn't imagine we would have been able to decipher his archaeological notations – what little I could still see resembled a cross between cuneiform and Ancient Egyptian demotic script, which have in common the fact that they don't look like any kind of language at all. Come to think of it, if you wanted to keep your work secret you could do worse than to write it in an ancient, dead language. Although the people most likely to be able to decipher it would be other archaeologists, so perhaps his writing wasn't encoded, just indecipherable.

He pulled out a pair of dividers and, using one point as a marker, moved it up and down the beach area, following my umpteenth rehearsal of my movements on that day in April. At last he made a mark in pencil and scrawled some remarks. He was not happy, however, and said so.

"I'll need to examine the area. How confident are you that you can take me back to the exact place where you found the object?"

I was not confident, but promised I would do my best. Over the course of the last two hours, Niall's polite manner had gradually ebbed away, following the tide of information, which didn't seem to be providing what he wanted. Strangely, this wasn't as annoying as it had been last night on the phone. (Perhaps I'm more tolerant of rudeness from beautiful people?)

At last, he announced brusquely that we would have to leave, "I can't be giving any more time to this now," and ushered us to the door.

He did recall himself sufficiently to thank me, and to ask for my phone number, and noted in his diary which days of the coming week were most suitable for us to show him the site of my find. We settled on Thursday. He retained the chess piece, but in return loaned us a CD-ROM about those Lewis Chessmen held in the Edinburgh museum. Sam, who had been almost silent throughout, spoke up: "Does that mean you think our queen *is* one of the Lewis chess pieces?"

Niall looked taken aback. "I thought I'd made that clear? This piece is very like those found on Lewis, although I need to do a lot more research to be able to say whether it was made by the same person or workshop. But it certainly appears to date from the same period."

He turned a stern eye on Sam, who was already glued to his every word. "This is an important discovery. I'll be able to tell you more the next time I see you." With that, the door closed behind us and we found ourselves wandering dazedly down the long street to the harbour, still slightly damp and ravenous.

I brought out some rather squashed ham sandwiches (thank goodness they didn't squash themselves all over the tea towel earlier) and we munched as we walked towards the ferry terminal. I glanced over at Sam. He had been remarkably quiet throughout our long interview, so much so that I was slightly worried about him. Apart from his question at the end, he had perked up only when I had credited him with the realisation of what our little queen was, and her possible authenticity. In fact, Sam seemed very pleased with himself, and his bad temper of the morning appeared to have melted away as his clothes had dried.

"Don't look a gift horse in the mouth," I told myself (and let sleeping dogs lie). Besides, I was enjoying a moment of quiet contemplation myself. It had been a long time since I'd experienced the surge of attraction I felt in the presence of Niall Webster. It was pleasant to think that, despite all the years of emotional numbness with Drew, I was still able to partake of such a normal human response. I told myself I had no interest in Niall Webster (too young, too pretty, too rude), but I basked in the warmth that spread through me as I relived the afternoon. Perhaps some changes I have thought of as a permanent result of growing up might turn out to be a self-protective reflex that I can overcome.

I tend to think of my future as being more of the same, only with less shouting in it. But maybe, just maybe, there was a chance things might get better. Not that the future would include jumping into bed with a bad-mannered archaeologist whom I'd only met once, but it was nice to be reassured that my body still had life in it.

Sam nudged me with his very bony elbow. "Penny for them."

I shook myself and smiled at him. I opened my mouth to make something up when he announced, "That was Ewan." Sure enough, he was waving his mobile phone at me. I must have been miles away not to notice him taking the call. "He can't take us till next week, so we'll go on Monday morning if the weather is okay. He says the tides are right and we might catch some mackerel. I've told him you want to go as well."

He stared at me challengingly. I looked back at him (feeling – well, what? Surprise I suppose) and thought for a moment. Sam had given the clear impression yesterday that this fishing trip was a chance to get away from me. What had changed between then and now? I had the feeling there were undercurrents here that I wasn't picking up on. Was Sam trying to placate me? Did he suddenly feel unsure of himself alone with Ewan? I shook myself mentally. (Life's hard enough without inventing anxieties, foolish woman.)

"I'd love to," I said.

7

Some kind of noise woke me. I rubbed my eyes, trying to focus on the clock. 5.30 a.m. Mmph. That's not even a time. I lay back and tried to work out what had disturbed my sleep. I'd been having that dream again – the one where I dream I'm awake, but can't open my eyes. Or sometimes, I wake and get out of bed, but can't switch the light on. I become conscious that my body is asleep, and that I must wake it or something terrible is going to happen.

Usually it degenerates into an ordinary nightmare – something about being chased, or eaten, or buried alive – but occasionally I go on dreaming that I am awake, knowing that I'm dreaming and powerless to help myself. I hate that one. Apart from anything else, it's very hard to be absolutely sure I am finally awake.

I rolled over and wrapped the pillow around my head, trying to pretend I was going back to sleep, but the noise came again. There. That was what woke me. Someone was in the kitchen.

As I groped under the bed for the jeans I'd dropped there a couple of days before, I realised the intermittent noise could be Sam. In the kitchen, before six in the morning? There must be something wrong.

When I got downstairs, I found him making scrambled eggs and toast. He'd set himself a place on the tiny kitchen table and turned to grab a second mug out of the cupboard as I came in.

"Hi, Mum, I couldn't sleep. Hope I didn't wake you."

"No worries," I said. "I wasn't sleeping very well either. What was bothering you?"

Sam plonked a mug of tea in front of me as I squeezed in between the table and the window.

"I had a nightmare about our chess queen," he said. "It started off being like a game of Battlechess, but then I realised it was being played on a beach and the pieces were bigger than me. Then she started shouting, and I got chased by all these knights and warders. I was running as fast as I could up a sand dune, but I kept slipping down again. They were just about to catch me when I woke up."

"Any idea what brought that on?"

"Dunno," said Sam, shoving an extra piece of bread into the toaster and splitting the eggs between two plates. "I mean, we gave our chess queen to Niall yesterday, so I suppose the dream was about her, but I don't know why it was bad."

"Sounds like a cross between Harry Potter and Alice in Wonderland," I told him. "And being chased by something you can't escape is a fairly standard nightmare."

"Yeah, I suppose so." Sam had his mouth full. It seemed that describing his dream had been enough to banish it. "What about yours?"

"Only something unpleasant that I don't really want to remember. Strange we both had nightmares – perhaps it was the curry we ate last night?"

"Mum, you are so sad."

"What are those piles of paper in the living room?"

"Um, school stuff. I've got this project for Geography. It has to be something to do with where I live, so I thought I might write about Calgary and the chess piece, but I don't really know what I'm going to do yet. There's some Maths stuff as well. I just want to get it out of the way so I can enjoy my holiday."

Wow. What a change from a couple of days ago. Perhaps our meeting with a real archaeologist has motivated him? I could do with a role model like that for my boy.

"I'm worried," I told him. "Boy voluntarily doing school work. Are you sure you feel okay?"

Sam favoured me with the kind of deeply scornful glance that is characteristic of teenagers all over the world. I bit my lip to stop myself from giggling.

"I think you're being very sensible. Let me know if you need any help with the Geography bit: I've got a few maps and guidebooks around, but I'm probably not much help on the Maths front."

"Don't worry, Mum." Sam teased. "Everybody knows men are better at Maths. Women's brains are not designed for logical thinking."

This was such a classic Drew remark that for a moment I was speechless. I could feel an offended reply rising to my lips but was forestalled when the phone rang. Sam's eyes met mine. He knew as well as I did that an early morning call was more likely to mean trouble at Nanna and Granddad's than anything else. He crossed the kitchen and answered the phone as I tried to squeeze back out from behind the kitchen table.

As he put the phone to his ear and spoke, his demeanour instantly changed. He glanced across at me, his shoulders hunching. Not Nanna and Granddad, then.

"Hello, Dad," he said.

I eased myself out from behind the table and sat on Sam's chair, making no attempt to take the receiver from him. What was Drew doing, phoning here? Sam was listening hard, not attempting to interrupt. "Yes," he said, and "Uh huh." Then, "Here, you can speak to her yourself."

"Hello, Drew."

"Ah, Cassandra." The expansive warmth of his voice told me someone else was listening. "Just trying to explain to Sam, but he felt it would be better if I spoke to you directly."

"What do you want?"

"An opportunity has come up that I believe would be of great benefit to Sam." In my mind's eye, I could see Drew's perfectly fitted suit, his immaculately manicured nails. He was probably examining the perfection of one hand while he held the phone in the other. He sounded particularly satisfied with himself.

"What kind of opportunity?"

"One of my business colleagues has a yacht. At the moment she is in a boatyard on the west coast of Scotland, being refitted. He has offered me the opportunity to take her out."

I could feel my hackles rising with each well-enunciated syllable. Even the most innocuous remarks, made in Drew's voice, could set my teeth on edge. "What has this got to do with Sam?"

"Of course, Sam will join me. It will be a great experience for him."

"Drew, are you talking about taking Sam away during his holiday? Because you already agreed Sam would come to me for the whole of summer break. I won't consent to him being taken out of school next term, either. It's an important year for him, and I don't want him going off on a sailing trip during school time. Is that what you're asking?" I broke off and stared out of the kitchen window, wondering why I let him make me so angry. I could hear my voice getting shriller with every sentence.

Drew's voice deepened a notch and became even more persuasive. "No, no, of course I'm not talking about term time. Education is very important, you know I support that." He definitely had someone with him. "This would be a valuable experience for Sam. Surely you aren't going to prevent him from taking up this chance?"

"When?"

"I don't have the dates yet. I'll know more once the yacht comes out of dry dock. I should be able to give the boy twenty-four hours warning."

"Twenty-four hours? Don't be ridiculous, Drew. You can't just phone up and expect Sam will drop his plans and go off with you at a day's notice. You've known about these holiday arrangements for months. What exactly is so great about this 'opportunity' you're offering him?"

"There are some people I'd like him to meet. They can

provide him with valuable experience."

"What people? Exactly who are we talking about?"

"Cassandra," the purr had the bite of steel behind it. "You can't expect me to share details of my personal life."

"Oh, so you're bringing the new girlfriend, then?"

Drew hissed in fury. I heard a sharp sound, as if he'd knocked over a piece of furniture, or maybe kicked it. I could almost smell his breath down the line as he spoke, all trace of the golden, persuasive voice gone. "That is none of your concern. I take it he will be ready when I call for him."

Sam had started forward, his hand outstretched to take the phone from me.

"Hang on, Drew. Sam wants to speak with you again."

"Then you'll have to explain to him why you made that impossible."

Sam's hand closed on the receiver just as I placed it back on its cradle. "No, wait. What happened? Did you hang up on him?"

"He hung up on me."

"Why?"

"He was angry with me. I'm sorry, Sam – I tried to tell him you wanted to talk to him. Do you want to call him back?"

"There isn't any point. He told me he was calling from a hotel, and that I should listen because he wouldn't say it twice. Even if I knew which hotel, he'd only be mad if I called him."

I sighed. Sam was probably right. "Did Dad tell you what it was about?"

"Yeah. He wants to take me on a yacht trip around the isles. For a few days, maybe a week."

Sam's posture seemed relaxed as he leaned against the doorjamb, but his eyes were anxious. "Mum, I'd really like to go. But I don't want to upset you."

I turned my back and filled the kettle with water while I got my expression under control. Drew brought out the worst in me, but there was no need for Sam to see any more of it than he had to. I turned back and smiled at him. "I don't see any reason for you not to go. Are you sure you want to? Dad didn't really give me any information about when, or where, or what you might need to take with you."

"He didn't tell me, either. But is it okay? I mean, if he rings up and says 'Come tomorrow', can I still go?"

"It'll be fine, honey. We can pack and get you down to the ferry in no time, and if you needed something on the voyage, I'm sure Dad could get it for you. There is one thing, though."

"What?"

"I expect you to have finished at least one of your school projects before you go. So you'd better get started."

I took my tea out into the garden, to give Sam space to get started on his schoolwork. I needed to get Drew out of my head too. The call had been irritating, but nothing out of the ordinary. I was more concerned to find out how he'd got hold of my phone number. The new number was unlisted precisely because of the trouble Drew had given me over the last few months, and I realised that now I would have to go through the whole process again.

As I walked through the door, something caught at my jeans. I looked down to see a thick bramble cane clawing at me. In fact, the whole garden was starting to look as though it was going back to the wild. I grabbed my secateurs from the porch windowsill and did for the blackberry, before settling down to pull out all the large weeds from the bed under the kitchen window. Once I'd made reasonable progress I stood up, wiping the dirt from my hands, and surveyed my domain.

The house (*my* house) stood on the corner of the main road and the drive leading to the big house, behind the trees. Its garden opened onto the loch, but my view was more homely. To my right the river chuckled, beyond the edge of the property, and to the left, across the road, a little stream leapt down from the hill: our source of water, reliable in all but the driest seasons because of the high level of rainfall here.

In front of me rose two storeys of corrugated iron elegance, topped with a slate roof. An unusual building material, probably associated more with sheds than houses, but mine is not the only house of its type on the island. It was shabby and in need of paint, and there were signs of rust where the downpipes don't channel the rain properly, but it was home. It had two dormer windows, partly set into the roof, and two lower ones, with a tiny porch between.

At a quick glance I saw several maintenance tasks that needed to be done, and looking up at my bedroom window reminded me that it's loose and lets in the rain. One of the problems with ironclad houses is that they lack insulation; my house is damp, draughty and very hard to keep warm. I love it anyway.

The garden is exactly the kind of muddle you'd expect from a summer home. A path straggles in to cross a rough pasture, in need of mowing now I'm keeping the gate closed and the sheep can't get in. There's a scatter of leggy shrubs and a moribund apple tree, none with branches lower than three feet above the ground (that's the deer). A stringy honeysuckle meanders up one side of the porch, but the only other flowers are some wild ox-eye daisies coming up in the lawn and an enormous patch of mint which has taken over the flowerbed beside the house.

The day the package arrived from my solicitor, containing the deeds to the house, I sat on the floor and cried. For days afterwards, I found myself stroking the windowsills or patting the kitchen bench; checking it was all still there, hardly able to believe it wasn't going to be taken away. But now that ownership has sunk it, I've begun to realise I will also have to start taking responsibility for the much needed and long overdue repairs. My home. My worries. Fantastic!

After scrubbing the dirt from under my fingernails, I stuck my head into the living room to see how Sam was getting on. He was already working, his head down and expression focused. I creaked the door to get his attention.

"All right?"

"Yeah. It's going okay."

"I'm off to Tobermory to get some shopping. You all right on your own?"

"Mmhmm."

Taking that as a positive response, I grabbed my car keys and headed out. Just as I opened the door I heard Sam call my name. I put my head round the door and looked at him.

"Mum, I just want you to know. It was me."

"What was you?"

"I told Dad your new number. I know I wasn't supposed to but he really sounded like he needed it, and I thought it would be okay. He can be persuasive, you know?"

"I know."

"It is okay, isn't it, Mum?"

"Of course it is. Don't you worry."

8

We picked up Niall off the first ferry, having pulled into a parking space opposite the terminal as the first vehicles began to make their way off the vessel. He strode through the oncoming crowd of visitors like a heron strutting its way through a field of geese. He was as good-looking as I remembered, with a Tilley hat clamped on his fair head and a khaki backpack with an impressive number of pockets. Sam scrambled into the back seat without being asked, much to my surprise. I'd expected him to put up a fight when he had to move (usually he sees the front passenger seat as his personal territory) but he was over and settled before I'd finished opening my mouth to ask him. The drive north was mostly silent, as my attempts to make conversation failed to draw in either of my passengers.

When I pulled up into the beach car park, I got out and stretched my back, leaving the other two to extricate themselves and Niall's gear. As expected, the archaeologist wanted to get down to business immediately. At first I took him to the spot where I thought I remembered finding the little queen. I bent down and showed him how the little hole had appeared in the sand, and I had inserted my fist in the space and felt the shape of the little figure. Then he made me walk up and down the beach, reliving in my own mind the course I had taken. I had to admit my mind had been wandering, and I had been paying little attention to my surroundings, but this reiteration made me far more certain when it brought me back to same place.

Niall pulled out a device that looked like an old mobile phone. It had a full-sized screen like an up-to-date mobile, but it was much too chunky. He held it up like a phone but didn't speak, instead making a notation in the margin of his field-map.

Sam was intrigued. "Is that GPS?" he asked. Niall turned towards him and Sam bent over the screen.

"My friend at school has a GPS app on his phone. Wouldn't that be easier?" Sam asked Niall. Niall didn't reply, but unzipped one of his other pockets, pulling out a slim mobile phone. He thumbed it on and turned the screen towards Sam. Sam looked at it and nodded in return.

"No signal," he said.

"That's one of the problems with the Highlands and Islands," said Niall. "Poor mobile phone coverage. Otherwise I could just have an app for everything and I wouldn't need so many pockets," he added, wryly. "The GPS has a built in booster, and I can usually get a signal if I'm patient."

I planted my bottom on a rock near the edge of the bay and looked out towards the horizon. I let my gaze slide round to where Niall and Sam were following the tide line, still deep in talk. Being here engendered feelings of serenity. This small bay in its sheltered position invites feelings of comfortable familiarity: it seems made to a human scale.

Not very long ago, only ten thousand years or so, the glaciers of the last Ice Age were still adding their thumbprint to the landscape, scouring and grinding their way across Scotland. At last, as the glaciers retreated, a thin wind-borne layer of white shell sand began to build up in this sheltered pocket on the north-west coast of Mull. There might have been people then: a handful of Mesolithic travellers stopping along the coast to flake a few flints or harvest from the sea. They are known from other places – Croig, Tenga – not far from here. But by and large the sand was allowed to build up, combining with fine loess blown on the wind from other places where glaciers had ground the land to silt and then retreated. A sparse habitat for grass and herbs carried in on the cold winds, the machair, came into existence.

Out on the Western Isles the machair is a rich and widespread habitat, whereas Calgary is only a small, though very precious, example. A crescent of sand, pale grey where the tide has ebbed, white flurries blowing across it, backed by a broad expanse of machair, rich with a diverse array of plant species. Once it was home, perhaps, to corncrake and curlew, lapwing and plover. It's hard to know, now, because after a few thousand years of silence people came again.

The builders of the little village up on the hill called it Caladh Ghearridh, the Bay of Good Pasture; or perhaps Caladh Airidh, Bay of the Summer Houses. Those who could have told us are all gone; cleared away in the eighteenth century to make room for sheep. The sheep in turn, joined by the ubiquitous rabbit, keep the machair shorn back to a scant web, which barely holds the sand together.

For a few weeks each year it is the Bay of Summer Houses again, as the impromptu camping ground at the west end of the bay fills up with tents, and the beach is thronged with people. They walk, they dig sandcastles, they light fires on the beach and roll down the dune slopes that edge the machair, and so the sheep-nibbled turf wears away. Once the people are gone, the storms of winter and the great tides of autumn and spring eat away at the weakened turf and bring it crashing down in lumps onto the shore, where it seeps away imperceptibly back into the beach.

I wandered seaward to a place where the sand had been packed firm by the retreating tide and squatted down. By the time the boys had finished their discussion I had completed the raised, stippled boss at the heart of a six-foot sunflower, and was beginning to mould the petals. I'd been right – Calgary's sand is a little too coarse for detailed sculpture – but I was enjoying myself. The sun beat down on the back of my neck and I pulled an old towelling sunhat out of my pocket and shoved it onto my head. Probably I started to hum. I do that when I'm contented.

In the middle of the fourth petal, a shadow fell across the work. I looked up to see Sam's skinny frame looming over me.

"Hungry yet?" he enquired hopefully. I stood and stretched – yes, I was hungry. It must be well past midday. "Go fetch Mr Webster," I said, "and I'll get the food."

I brought out the picnic from under the shade of the car and carried it over to the edge of the machair. I watched the two males as I laid out the sandwiches and other picnicky stuff. They seemed to be having a serious conversation, but Sam suddenly laughed and Niall grinned in response. For a moment his face lit up and his eye caught mine as he glanced towards me. Sam sat down next to me and picked up a cherry tomato. As he bit into it the juice squirted everywhere and he turned away, embarrassed. Niall caught my eye again. Was that an actual twinkle?

"I've been trying to make sense of this," I said, as I attempted to balance the mugs in the sand with one hand and unscrew the top of the thermos with the other. "I know you said we'd found something of real interest, but what exactly did you mean? We can't have found one of the real Lewis Chessmen, surely?"

Niall nodded seriously and began to talk around a mouthful of bread. "The weight, condition and complex decoration of your piece feel authentic," he said. "Your queen is not exactly like any individual piece held in either the British Museum or the Museum of Scotland. But it displays a large number of similarities in style and design. That rather argues in favour of authenticity. Even a really good copy, or a competent forgery, would be expected to more closely resemble the known pieces. The combination of brocaded drapery and the geometric carving on the throne is unlike any of the known examples. And as you've noticed, her expression is unique. "

"Uniquely grumpy," interjected Sam.

"I only know of two other chess pieces of similar age and style to the Uig hoard, and both were found in Norway: a broken queen, found during a dig at the old Archbishop's palace in Trondheim, and a king found on a nearby island."

"Norway! But that's even further away than Lewis. Can it

really have drifted from there?"

"Oh no, definitely not. It's in remarkably good shape for its age. It can't have been directly exposed to water for very long, or we would have seen a much greater degree of cracking and wear. It seems to me most likely it was deposited in situ, or very close to where you found it. Hence our search today."

"I didn't think the Vikings had very much to do with Mull," I said, but Sam interrupted fiercely.

"Stop saying Vikings, Mum. You're two hundred years too late. Isn't she?" Appealing to Niall with both eyebrows raised, his clear grey eyes fixed on the archaeologist. Niall nodded.

"In a sense you are both right." He broke off a bit of crust and chewed it slowly, then put the rest down and delivered a lecture. "The height of Viking raiding was around 800AD. That was the period when the monasteries began to be abandoned, and anyone who lived near the coast of Northern Britain went in fear of the summer raiders.

"By the end of the ninth century, many of the islands of the Hebrides had become home to Norse settlers. They were a powerful force in the Outer Isles. The language and records of the people who lived there were virtually obliterated, and replaced with Norse language and customs. Even though those islands later became a stronghold of the Gaelic language, you can still hear that Norse heritage in their names, and in many loan words.

"Recent DNA studies in Orkney have shown that it's highly likely that Norse settler/raiders disposed of virtually all the male inhabitants, but left the women alive and at home. Many of the present day male inhabitants have been shown to have had Norse ancestors, but mitochondrial DNA, passed down in the female line, comes from the earlier inhabitants of the islands, perhaps even from the original hunter-gatherers who settled there thousands of years ago."

"Mitre-what DNA?" I said.

"Mitochondrial. In every cell of your body are little

organelles called mitochondria, which are the powerhouses of the cell, helping us to utilise the energy we get from our food. Mitochondria have their own DNA, different from the genetic material in our chromosomes, and it's always passed down from mother to child. It lets us study matrilineal inheritance patterns more readily than patrilineal ones."

"All right, that does ring a bell."

"Sam, did you understand it too? Just tell me if you want me to explain what I'm talking about."

"Yeah, I'm fine. I already knew what mitochondrial DNA was." Sam helped himself to a handful of crisps and lay on his back, feeding them into his mouth one at a time. To a stranger he might appear uninterested in what Niall had to say, but he turned his head slightly towards the speaker, and stopped chewing whenever Niall was talking.

"Norse leaders had a stronghold in the Isle of Man and others in Ireland. Ships must have gone regularly up and down this whole coast. In 1050AD, Edgar of Scotland ceded the Sudreyjar to Magnus III of Norway: that is, the Isle of Man and all the Inner and Outer Hebrides. There's even a legend that Magnus stood at the helm of a ship while it was dragged across the isthmus of Tarbert, Kintyre, to prove he could 'sail' right round it, and thus claim it as another island possession. The islands didn't become Scottish again until after the Treaty of Perth in 1263AD—"

I interrupted. "What about the Lords of the Isles? I thought they were around at about the same time as the Lewis Chessmen were made – middle of the twelfth century. Could our piece have anything to do with them?"

"Well, technically the Lords of the Isles didn't begin their reign until well into the thirteenth century. The Lewis Chessmen were dated to the later part of the twelfth century, and if our piece is from the same period it's a wee bit too early. Somerled was the ancestor of the Lords of the Isles, and he died in 1164. He left several sons, and the Lordships of the Isles eventually rose out of their conflicts. So our piece could potentially be associated with the sons of Somerled."

That was plenty to think about, and the three of us sat and worked our way through apples and cake while it sank in. Niall did justice to the food and drank his fair share of my homemade lemonade as well as tea, but his thoughts were clearly not on the meal. He kept glancing around, frowning, as if he could make an archaeological marvel appear out of the sand hills by sheer willpower. I had the feeling his eagle-eyed gaze would not miss any clue to past use of the area. It was with present, living inhabitants that he seemed to have trouble.

"Where are your family from?" I asked him.

He glanced back at me, and made an effort. "My parents live in Devon," he said.

"Oh, lovely. Are they near the sea?"

"No, they're on the edge of Dartmoor."

"Do you visit them often?"

"No."

I gave up and took another sandwich. It was Sam's turn to take up the conversation.

"What do you do when you're not working?" he asked.

Niall gazed blankly at my son. "Oh, this and that," he said.

It was hopeless. Sam subsided and Niall gave every impression of being deep in thought.

After filling us up with facts about local history, he went back to being only half-aware of our presence. It seemed as though, to Niall, I was only a marker, a potential signpost to the reality he was hoping to unearth. I had never met anyone so single-minded about his work (I might equally say 'his life').

While I cleared up and Sam drank the last of the lemonade, Niall rose abruptly and wandered back to the place where I believed I had found the chess piece. He turned a little sideways and kicked at the sand cliff with the side of his foot, then looked down to see the results of his action. When he noticed me watching, he turned away sheepishly. I'm sure that isn't an approved excavation technique.

Niall reverted to type, and pulled a notepad out of his backpack. He also retrieved a long plastic box, which turned out to contain the pieces of a small metal detector. With this assembled, he began to sweep the area, beginning at the point where the picnic basket still stood and, using it as a marker, slogged up and down the beach. He covered the beach in two-metre swathes, marked out with driftwood branches, stopping only to stretch his aching back. As far as I could see, he intended to keep going until nightfall.

I sat in the sun and watched him, while Sam made a half-hearted attempt on the sunflower sculpture. Soon his enthusiasm was captured, and he settled down to complete the flower and its leaf. I stirred myself to make a butterfly, alighting on the flower, but the coarse sand defied my efforts and I conceded defeat. It was far too hot for anyone but fanatical archaeologists to be working.

Sam finished carving the last leaf vein and leaped towards the sea. I opened my mouth to warn him, but swallowed the words back. In the presence of another adult (even the to-all-appearances unconscious presence of Niall) I didn't want to nag. Let him find out for himself. Sam did. He charged into the sea, and straight back out again, hardly more than damp above the knee. "It's freezing," he shouted. "It's supposed to be summer."

I walked towards him, trying not to show that I was laughing.

"It's always cold," I reminded him. "You've been here before."

Sam's face was rueful. "I never remember," he muttered. "It looks so shiny and blue, and the sun is so hot, and I always think it's going to be warm."

"Someone told me once there are people who swim in the sea here, even in the winter, but they're all over seventy. Modern man has become too soft."

"Mum?"

"Yes, Sam?" I replied warily, responding to something in his tone.

"Do you remember the beach at Granddad's farm? We used to do heaps of sand sculptures, and then we'd run into the sea to cool off. It was always warm."

I remembered. For a moment, Calgary's white beach disappeared, and under my feet was the hot, yellow sand of Huna Cove. I remembered day after day of summer sunshine: running down to the sea with Sam in the mornings, then home again in the evenings to wolf down whatever Nanna had prepared for us. I felt a twinge of guilt – even then, Nanna and Granddad had been old, and yet I continued to take it for granted that I could always go home. How long was it since I had last spoken to them? Too long. I vowed to call as soon as I could.

"Mum?"

Sam's voice recalled me to myself. "Well," I said, "you have to remember their farm was at a much lower latitude than we are here – more like the southern hemisphere equivalent of Provence than Mull. Nearly all the times we spent there were summer holidays, so you're remembering the best of the year. There was plenty of hail, sleet and snow in the winters. Do you remember the time we were snowed in, and Granddad helped you make a snow horse? We were reading *Moominland Midwinter* at the time."

Sam didn't. Too many British winters and snowmen had covered that memory, although he did recall Granddad borrowing his toy bells and shaking them outside the window at midnight on a hot and windy Christmas Eve, pretending he was Santa Claus. Granddad had never been able to adequately explain how Santa's sleigh could travel without snow.

Our New Zealand Christmases had started at dawn (about 4 a.m. for Nanna), and then off to the beach for an all-day picnic. Nanna would be busy in the kitchen all morning, but even she packed it in when it got really hot and came down in her flowered dress and a new straw hat (a new one every Christmas from Granddad, since the year they'd married) to sit under the big umbrella and direct proceedings.

Drew would appear mid-afternoon, ambling unwillingly down to the sea and hanging about, hoping someone would relent and find him a drink. One year he had brought his own. He'd got one beer down before Grandpa spotted the chillibin and quietly poured the lot away. There had been no words spoken. Drew knew Granddad would have no alcohol on the farm. No exceptions.

"You're woolgathering again," Sam's voice roused me. "Mum, what time is Niall's ferry?"

I started when I looked at my watch. "Quickly!" I pushed Sam. "Go and get him. I'll grab the gear and we might just make it." This was critical, as the 5 p.m. ferry was the last one today, and I was sure Niall had said he was only coming for the day. Sam raced off down the beach as I gathered up the picnic basket and the blanket. The sunflower was left in solitary splendour to await the incoming tide. I reached the car just as Niall thundered up, his face perspiring, but with rage, not effort. "Why did you move the basket? I was using that as my start-marker. Now I don't know where I began the first sweep!"

I looked at him in bemusement. I had forgotten he'd been using the basket to mark his metal-detecting sweeps. "I'm sorry," I said, "but what about the ferry?"

"The ferry? Oh my God." Niall stared at me as I began to shove the picnic things into the boot. He grabbed his pack and, stowing the metal detector in its case, jumped into the back of the car. Sam came puffing up and climbed into the front, and we pulled away.

65

9

I drove as fast as I dared on the rough, single-track roads, and nearly ended up in the ditch when we came round a corner and found a tractor and trailer trying to occupy the same space as us. We made better speed when we joined the two-way road at Aros, but reached the ferry terminal in Craignure in time to see the bow door closing as the ferry pulled away from the link-span. An intense wave of disappointment swept over me, conscious that I'd let Niall down. I straightened my shoulders and reminded myself I was not responsible for other people – he would have to look after his own interests. Niall was unperturbed. "I'll stay in a B&B somewhere," he said. "If I can get one near Calgary, I'll be able to do some more work tonight."

I resisted the urge to point out that he couldn't expect me to keep running him round indefinitely, but settled instead for the non-negotiable reality. "You won't find anywhere. It's the week of the Mull and Iona Food Festival and you'll not get a bed for love or money. You'd best stay with us."

"That won't be necessary. I'll find something."

"Suit yourself," I said, shortly. "The tourist office will help you find somewhere to stay." Sam and I went into the village shop, while Niall and his backpack disappeared into the building Calmac shares with the tourist office. Sam settled himself into the front of the car and perused the Oban Times while we waited.

"Look at this, Mum. It's about our chessman."

"What does it say?"

"Buried Treasure on Isle of Mull. Buried treasure has been found at Calgary Bay, on the north-west coast of the Isle of Mull.

Dr. Niall Webster, spokesman for Argyll and the Isles Archaeological Survey, confirmed that an object has been found, believed to date from the early Middle Ages. Dr. Webster would not reveal to this reporter the actual nature of the treasure. However, he went on to say that 'there is no guarantee of further finds, but we cannot rule it out.'

Local police on Mull have no information at this time. They have been unable to confirm whether the find comes under the category of 'treasure trove', which would likely be confiscated by the Crown."

Sam read the article out loud, then flicked through the paper looking for other items of interest. "I suppose it had to be Niall," he said. "He's practically the only person they've got in Oban."

This was true. In our lunchtime semi-conversation, I had ascertained that Niall ran the Oban office with the help of a secretary/ receptionist/ cleaner who worked twenty hours a week. There were other AIAS personnel currently working in Skye and Islay, but the whole unit had only half a dozen permanent staff. I had expressed surprise that such a small concern could afford the high-tech gear I had seen Niall using: not only the GPS-equipped mobile phone and the metal detector, but also his up-to-the-minute laptop and some of the other gear which had been scattered around the Oban office. Niall had looked uncomfortable, and admitted that some of it belonged to him personally. (Curiouser and curiouser. There's more to Mr Webster than meets the eye.)

The rear passenger door opened and the man himself climbed in. "You were right," he said. "There's nothing. May I take you up on your kind offer?"

"Of course." Privately, I thought he would do better to adopt that pleasant tone all the time, rather than turn it on only when he wanted something, but I said nothing more, and the journey was soon over. As we made our way to the front door, Sam remembered the newspaper article and showed it to Niall.

"Shit! Where's my mobile? I must make some calls. Oh, the idiots. I told them not to say there might be anything more to find. Oh God, I can't get a signal."

I put my hand on his arm, trying to calm his agitation. "You can't use your mobile here. This little valley doesn't get any kind of signal. But come inside and you can use my landline."

Niall allowed himself to be led into the house, and spent over an hour making a series of frantic phone calls. He sounded like a desperate general trying to mobilise troops for a sudden offensive. I couldn't imagine what was upsetting him so much, but busied myself making up the spare bed and putting together some pasta and salad. I felt smug about having made bread the day before, even though as far as I had known only Sam and I were going to be eating it. Sam laid the table and even filled a vase with some of the big daisies from the garden, which delighted me. He doesn't often think to make gestures like that, and I loved him for it. He seemed taken aback when I thanked him for his thoughtfulness, but suffered me to kiss his cheek before taking himself off on a fridge raid.

We all enjoyed the meal, and Niall and I were starting to wash the dishes when Sam arrived in the kitchen.

"Niall?"

Niall looked round at him.

"So you reckon our chess piece probably came from Norway?"

"Let's look at what we know. Our piece is very similar in material, construction and design to the Lewis Chessmen. So it's reasonable to conclude that it comes from the same period in time."

Sam nodded. As he spoke, Niall gesticulated with the mug he was drying, tea towel hanging forgotten from his other hand.

"Some aspects of the design of the Lewis chessmen have led to speculation that they were made in workshops in Trondheim. This is supported by the finds in Trondheim itself. Others think it more feasible that they were made in Iceland, the most likely source of the ivory. Also, by the middle eleven hundreds Iceland had been settled and was importing a huge array of goods including luxury goods such as wine and beer, wax, honey, cloth and metals. The main port supplying Iceland was Trondheim, but they brought in supplies from all over the Norse world, including Ireland and the Sudreyjar.

"Incidentally, Norway also exported timber here. Nearly all the timber used for boat-building in the Hebrides was sourced from Scandinavia. It was possible to import a whole boat for assembly at destination."

"Medieval Ikea," said Sam, smirking. Niall looked at him sideways and he subsided.

"Many of the Hebrides bear the marks of Norse language. Even the work 'mull' means a high plateau, and from the sea the northern part of Mull appears to be exactly that. There are many names with Norse affiliations, such as names ending with 'aig', which likely comes from the Norse 'vik', meaning a harbour. It's also recorded that Icelandic traders erected a beacon on Sanday in 1200AD. Sanday is in the Orkney Islands, which doesn't prove they came as far south as this, but it definitely isn't on the route to Trondheim!

"In any case, the Lewis Chessmen date from around 1150-1200AD, so they represent the middle part of the period of Norse occupation of the Hebrides. Their presence suggests the existence in Lewis of a powerful, rich elite, able to import rare and costly luxuries. It should not come as a surprise to think such people might also have been living on the Inner Hebrides. As you know, this is where the Lords of the Isles arose in the twelfth century. Their ancestor was Somerled, which means 'the summer leader': a Viking name, if I ever heard one.

"There's even been a case made recently, based on textual analysis of the Icelandic Sagas as well as some excavation, that the Lewis Chessmen may actually have been made in a workshop in Iceland."

"Can I ask a question?" Sam had a frown on his face. "How

do we know the dates of the Lewis Chessmen? Were they carbon dated?"

"Actually, that's an interesting question."

Sam looked pleased. He leaned against the doorframe and folded his arms.

"We know they couldn't have come into existence before 1150AD. That is because all the bishops are wearing the mitre facing forwards on their heads, not sideways. That didn't happen until after the middle of the twelfth century. In fact, the Lewis Chessmen are the earliest surviving example of the bishop-piece in chess.

"Some of the knights have round helmets, of the kind called chapels-de-fer or iron caps. Helmets like this are depicted on some seals from the late-twelfth and thirteenth centuries.

"The stylistic designs carved on the backs of the thrones of the kings and queens are also broadly similar to stonework carvings on a number of Scandinavian churches. This is the Romanesque style of art and architecture, sometimes also called the twelfth-century Renaissance, when Europe was flooded with newly-discovered Classical Greek and Roman texts, which had been preserved in Arabic translations, prompting a flowering of intellectual and artistic achievement.

"The combination of all these factors dates the Lewis Chessmen to a very brief period – no longer than fifty years at the end of the twelfth century. The other examples known from Scandinavia, and our find, all fit within the same period, I'm certain of that."

Niall waited for a moment, to see if there would be any more questions. Sam just nodded, and after a moment Niall turned to me. "May I ask you something?

"Of course."

"I have fully comprehensive insurance to drive any vehicle. We need it, really, in AIAS. You never know what you might be called on to drive."

I waited for him to get to the point. Sam pinched a handful

of raisins from the cupboard and headed back into the living room.

"I wonder if you would allow me to borrow your car. That would enable me to go back to Calgary, while the light lasts, and continue my survey. I'd like to get as much as possible done before the morning, but I don't want to have to ask you to drive me out there again."

I thought about it. While I wasn't entirely keen to lend my car to someone I hardly knew, I had no intention of acting as chauffeur again. I briefly considered sending Sam as a chaperone, but decided that if I couldn't trust Niall on his own with my car then it would definitely not be a good idea to send Sam off with him. I nodded. "Okay, that's fine. There should be enough petrol."

"I'll pay for fuel, of course. Thank you."

Once he'd gone, I left Sam flicking through freesat channels and went out for a run, feeling I needed to clear my head before facing whatever Niall had organised for tomorrow. I took the road for a couple of miles, turned into the forest track at West Ardhu and jogged for half an hour up the mossy path beside the little stream that joins ours further down the valley. I crossed the road onto the open hillside then hauled myself up the last stretch onto the big boulder that juts out from the hill. I could see right across the forest block to Loch Cuin, calmness personified in the late evening light.

I sat for a few minutes letting the quiet seep into me, and then started back down again. As I reached the top of the forest track, I was met by a wet and very smelly dog. Molly sniffed me and gave me an enthusiastic lick. I turned my head and there was Ewan, striding down the road towards the forest edge. "Going my way?"

He fell in with me and we jogged on together. I noticed Ewan's silence didn't bother me – I was used to it. It wasn't often we had a long conversation. (Have we ever? I might have to think hard to recall one.) Unlike Niall's monosyllabic replies

71

and obvious distraction, Ewan's silence seemed a part of him. I'd met Ewan through Hector, right here on Mull, though I saw him only occasionally in the summer, usually when Drew wanted to hire a vessel or go fishing.

It's only since I moved here permanently that I've found myself bumping into him more often, and when we met once on a run it seemed sensible, as well as pleasant, to run together. I glanced to my right, noting his profile, and realising suddenly that I found myself attracted to him. Here was a well-known face with a mystery behind it. I know so little about what goes on inside that quiet head, although we have spent many pleasantly uncomfortable hours running in all weathers and terrains.

He's very tall, lean and rangy, with a lined and weather-beaten face. When I'm with him I find myself talking less, and it makes me aware of the continuous commentary going on in my head all the time, often hyper-critical, much of it in Drew's voice. To be fair, I had my inner critic before I met Drew, but these days he definitely has ownership of it. Being with Ewan calms the little voice, and running helps too, so the combination works wonders.

By the time we reached my drive, I felt great; mind peaceful and body tired, just the right combination to help me sleep well. I waved goodbye to Ewan and Molly as I turned in.

"See you on Monday."

Ewan raised a hand in reply and ran on.

10

Dawn arrived with a burst of birdsong and the rustle of leaves. I could smell the honeysuckle outside my window as the first warmth of the sun reached it and woke its scent. It was the kind of morning that made me glad to be alive, but not in a hurry to do anything about it. I was sure if I thought about it I could come up with a good reason to get up, so I decided not to think about it. I lay in snuggled comfort, stretching my toes under the covers, and listened to the birds' joyful chorus.

I could hear faint sounds from downstairs – I'd been aware of noises late last night when Niall came in, and guessed he'd used all the long hours of light and half-light to keep searching the beach. He couldn't have had much rest. I sighed, and threw back the covers. Much as I'd like to lie in, I needed to get up and look after our guest.

Niall appeared as I was making a pot of tea, looking tired and tousled, and accepted a mug without speaking. We made our way into the living room and sat in companionable silence, not bothering to make conversation, until Sam also staggered out to join us. I got up to make toast and heard the two of them talking quietly. When I came out with jam and homemade marmalade they set to, and soon cleared up all the food I could provide. It seems that while men may have mostly stopped growing by their twenties, they still require the same vast amount of food as teenagers.

"Niall is going out again as soon as his mates come across on the first ferry. Can I go with him? He says he's going to be out there all day. They're going to do magnetic resonance scanning. Please, Mum?"

"I'll do a deal with you, Sam. If you go up now and spend

three hours on your school report, I'll run you out to the beach mid-morning."

Sam agreed reluctantly, but I knew he would accept it as a fair deal. He went straight off to get started, which endeared him to me still further. I was dreading a whiny argument in front of our visitor, and perhaps Sam had felt the same way. Not for the first time, I reflected on the value of good male mentors for teenage boys, especially ones whose own attitudes were nearer to what I want for Sam. Niall might be somewhat lacking in personal communication skills, but he didn't seem to be a bad role model. At least he was well educated and gainfully employed, two of the great hopes I have for Sam's future. Niall's friends soon turned up, in two very battered Land Rovers, and he scrambled into the back of one with his gear and disappeared without a backwards glance.

I left Sam working and went for a walk. Meeting Ewan last night had reminded me it had been a long time since I'd popped over to visit Hector. As I walked down the road I remembered my first meeting with the old man, all those years ago.

I'd unpacked all the family's belongings into the new summer house and obsessed a bit about how I was going to feed us from the tiny, ill-equipped kitchen. Day one was going to be fine; we were intending to head out to the pub for dinner, but I didn't want to have to go out every day. I couldn't do anything about it until Drew came back with the car, so I went for a walk instead, to see what kind of I place I found myself in.

I was deep in thought about the merits of grill pans versus toastie makers, and wondering whether I would be able to buy either of them in Tobermory, when I realised I was passing the gate to a paddock. Leaning on the gate was an elderly man, with an equally elderly, grey-muzzled dog sitting beside him. "Good morning." I said.

He nodded and raised his cap. "A lovely morning," he replied.

The old-fashioned courtesy won my heart, and I stopped to fondle the dog's ears and exchange some more chat about the island and its weather. Hector was calm, pleasant and easy to talk to. I discovered he could be found leaning on his gate most mornings in fine weather, although if the weather was bad he tended to stay in and let Molly go out with his son.

Our second summer on Mull, I went looking for him as soon as I arrived. That day he was nowhere to be seen, but a couple of days later there he was, leaning on his gate as though he had never been away. A week or so later, he invited me in for tea. Sam was well behaved, and immediately formed a bond with the dog.

That was the first time I met Ewan, although he made off to his caravan as quickly as politeness would allow. A few weeks later, when Drew announced he was taking us all fishing, I met Ewan again, as the skipper of *Martha-Margaret* and Drew's slave for the day.

Ewan made no objection to Drew's high-handed behaviour, but remained polite and aloof. Even when Drew lost his temper at his continuing failure to catch anything, humiliated by Sam's growing pile of fish, and snapped at Ewan in genuine rudeness, Ewan kept his cool. He calmly picked up the thrown rod, untangled the line and rebaited it, and handed it to me without so much as a raised eyebrow.

He ducked into the cabin and opened a tall locker, bringing out an alternative rod for Drew who, mollified by what he saw as properly deferential behaviour, settled down and finally managed to land something. Ewan left him to it, and went to help Sam land his latest catch. Later he cooked up a feast of mackerel, potato and onion, which was exactly what a day of fresh air and salt water fishing called for. He handed me my plate with a courteous diffidence and the faintest hint of a smile. The man had said virtually nothing all day. It was an exercise in the subtle eloquence of silence that I've never forgotten.

Hector wasn't home, and the door was locked. That was unusual (in summer, the doors were usually wide-open to the weather) and it probably meant he'd gone away for the day. I didn't mind – I'd enjoyed the walk, and it had allowed me to put off my new proofreading assignment for a bit longer. When I got back to the house, Sam was ready with Maths papers in hand. I signed and returned them and Sam stuffed them into an envelope and hastily sealed it.

"Can we go now?"

I gathered myself together and pulled on my walking boots, while Sam hurled himself into the car. We posted the assignment at an isolated post-box en route, and rattled on to Calgary. When we got there, I was amazed. There was no room to park in the beach car park: it was full of vehicles, and the beach and machair were swarming with people, many of them using metal detectors or other mysterious bits of equipment. Pairs and small groups of people were quartering the machair, heads down in concentration, or making notes on clipboards, in books or on scraps of paper.

I squeezed my car onto the verge, hoping the patch of ground between the road and the ditch was as firm as it seemed. Sam was out and away before I'd turned off the engine, having spotted Niall in a huddle with two other people. Sam ran over, shouting Niall's name, and joined the group. They looked up as I walked across the machair towards them.

"It's as I feared," Niall said. "People have read that newspaper article and come to try their luck. Most people don't realise that if they find anything really important, it won't belong to them, and they'll have to hand it over to the crown. I've told them if they think they've found something, they must call one of us over at once, before they try to dig. Of course, anything they remove from its find site immediately loses its context, and is of far less value archaeologically. We must be able to see every item in situ."

I felt myself flush with embarrassment. Surely he hadn't

expected me to leave the little queen where I had found it? Niall seemed completely unaware of my reaction, and continued ranting about amateurs disturbing sites of potential value (archaeological value, presumably) and waving his arms at the army of eager gold-diggers around him. I came to the conclusion that he wasn't talking about me, and decided it was best not to remind him that I'd removed an object from its context. After all, ignorance might be an even greater sin in Niall's book than deliberate damage. I resisted the urge to get into an argument with him about 'treasure hunters'; I'm pretty sure the finder of treasure does have some rights. Instead I smiled politely, made my excuses, and left Sam to uphold the family's honour.

I had originally intended to return home and get back to work, but the weather was too good to waste, so I set off around the bay towards the road. I had a bag full of fresh scones, and I thought I knew who might appreciate a share of them. I intended to walk right around the coast, and back over the Torloisk hill road. A walk of some four hours: that should give Sam plenty of time to expend his archaeological enthusiasm. As I passed the head of the beach, I heard a shout. A grey-haired man wearing an AIAS sweatshirt was waving to Niall's group. He was standing beside a metal detector-carrying couple, all of them wearing expressions of excitement and anticipation. Niall loped over, closely followed by Sam.

As I turned away and trudged up the road, I couldn't help but contrast this busy, noisy, crowded scene with winter walks at Calgary, when I was frequently the only human soul in the picture, surrounded by silence apart from my sand-shuffling footsteps, the cry of oystercatchers and the ever present shush of wind and sea in my ears. Even the day I found the chess queen had been marked by only one other group of humans: the young family taking an early Easter holiday.

I recalled my loneliness and aimless lack of purpose last winter, moving from empty house to empty beach and back, feeling as though I'd never have a sense of aspiration again. What a contrast to the last few days. I'd been so busy and interested that I'd had no time to feel sorry for myself. I wondered what activities I could find to keep myself busy when Sam went back to school.

I climbed steadily for a few minutes and then, as I turned the headland, the hubbub died away and the still clearness of summer air enveloped me. A slight sea-breeze sprang up, and I tucked my hair behind my ears, although it blew straight out again. I stopped and gazed north-west over the vast, blue ocean, feeling the heat of the sun strike square between my shoulder blades, as palpable as a physical blow.

The mountains of Rum were a little to the right of my view, with a hazy hint of Skye's Cuillins behind, and the tiny lumps of Muck and Eigg in front. If I turned slightly to my left, I could see the long, low shape of Coll, with its white beaches. Straight ahead the sea stretched unbroken to the Western Isles, the land of summer: Tir nan Og; a mystical realm where most people still speak Gaelic, and where the selkies still shed their skins and come ashore to meet with mortal folk. At least, so said a lively part of my imagination. I'd never been to those islands, and in a way, I didn't want to. I preferred to preserve my romantic illusions.

As I stood watching, a small shape intruded: Caledonian MacBrayne's *Lord of the Isles*, making the thrice-weekly ferry run from Oban to Barra and South Uist. The ferry seemed tiny on that immensity of water, and I suddenly saw it as a small bird sailing on a wide sky, blithely unaware of the vast depth of space beneath its keel. The voyage it had begun was the same as that made for thousands of years by people searching for a better place to live, for wealth and status, to trade or invade, or just to see the world.

Anywhere that can be reached on a calm day, will be. The vast sweep of the Pacific, with its myriad of tiny islands, was settled by brave Polynesians who set off eastward, always sure they would find another land, following only their hearts, the spoken knowledge of their ancestors and the signposts of seabirds, ocean currents and cloud patterns. At last, they reached New Zealand, and Hawaii, and Easter Island, and so stitched together the greatest body of water on the globe into a patchwork of human dispersal. All over the world, places have been settled, raided or just plain visited because they can be, and because we humans are a curious species.

I shaded my eyes against the glare off the sea, and thought about ocean distances in the world of the Lewis Chessmen. Sometimes I find it difficult to imagine what life must have been like back then. Post-industrial revolution Britain is such a different place from even three or four hundred years ago, let alone a thousand. But here in the Hebrides it isn't so hard to picture. Life would still have to go on, whatever the weather, so that houses could be built, food provided and necessities produced or traded for. People would have been waiting for the regular visits of ships to provide what they couldn't grow or make for themselves.

The only difference now is that the sailing birlinns have been replaced by powered vessels. The ferries are still the life-blood of the islands, and even tourism is nothing particularly new. Samuel Johnson, he of the dictionary, and his friend Boswell visited Mull and Ulva, and there were plenty of others like them. The basics of life have remained comfortingly familiar, despite all our technological advancements.

11

My reverie had taken me right round the coast road and up onto the bleak bog-lands of Treshnish. I tramped onwards, feeling the muscles in my legs stretch and loosen, and trying to ignore my nose. It always runs when I run. Good old walking boots – I've had them for years and they have moulded perfectly to my feet. I should have been wearing these on the day at Calgary when I found the chess piece.

The ever-present sheep were scattered about in small bands, and the road meandered among island boulders emerging from oceans of cotton grass and bog rush. The fluffy white heads of the cotton grass alternated with patches of well-grazed turf but, here and there, wild flowers had evaded the sheep. Delicate heads of harebell nodded, Scottish bluebell, blue on blue, and a whole clump of tall oxeye daisies jutted from a gap in the rocks.

A hoarse croak came from overhead, and I glanced upwards to see a pair of ravens wheeling and posturing above me. Overhead, the blue vault of heaven stretched away forever, but on the horizon a pinkish haze danced. I sat myself down on a roadside boulder to take a swig from my water bottle, and was pulling myself to my feet when I heard a vehicle. I didn't bother to look round, assuming it would pass me, but the battered Volvo estate pulled up alongside. The passenger door opened and a familiar voice enquired, "Hiya, Cas. Coming in for tea?"

I climbed into the car, shoving aside the litter on the seat, and swivelled round to say "Hello" to Tilly, ensconced in her car seat with three dolls and a small but very hairy dog for company. Tilly ignored my overtures, but Dogger acknowledged me with a friendly yawn. I grinned at the driver:

"Long time no see."

Bernie grinned back, and shoved the car into gear. With a protesting screech it capitulated and we moved off. After a few minutes, we turned left onto the farm track, and the jolting, bone-jarring journey put an end to any opportunity for conversation. We drew up outside a classic Mull farmhouse: white-painted plaster topped with grey tile, a stark two-storey rectangle relieved by two dormer windows and a riotous profusion of nasturtiums and roses, in clashing colours, scrambling all over the front porch. It was the kind of house that would have been built for the factor or tacksman, back in the days of absentee lairds and tenant farmers. Now it housed the noisy, cheerful brood of Kavanaghs: Jed, Bernie, Tom and Tilly the human ones, along with innumerable cats, Dogger, the farm dogs and occasional boxes of orphaned chicks, lambs, or baby rabbits.

Bernie heaved her hugely pregnant bulk out of the car and kneaded the small of her back. I moved around to do it for her.

"Oh, that's heavenly. You should do it for a living."

"I can't afford the liability insurance." I was only half joking.

"Come in and set yourself down. I've got three kinds of herb tea, or instant coffee. You'll have to make do with rich tea biscuits."

"I'll have whatever you're having, and I'll contribute a slightly crumbly bag of scones."

"You're an angel from heaven. I've always said so."

I fell into a low, shapeless armchair, and immediately acquired a cat and Tilly, equipped with a handful of picture books. I turned the pages and suffered my hair to be minutely inspected by tiny fingers, while Tilly told herself the stories and Bernie kept up a continuous stream of chat until the tea was ready. Tilly was bribed away with a bit of scone and orange juice, and Bernie laid herself full-length on the old sofa. I watched her with sympathy.

"How's Tiny?"

Bernie groaned and ran her fingers through her hair. Bernie's bump had inevitably become 'Tiny', after the third member of the Tots TV characters. Bernie swore that when they had named their children (Tom, after his Granddad, and then Matilda after Bernie's Mum) they had never heard of the program, but Tilly, Tom and Tiny they had become regardless.

"Tiny is huge, and if he/she/it doesn't make an appearance soon I think I'm going to burst!"

"Are you sure it isn't twins?"

"Shut up. Don't tempt fate." Bernie looked suitably shocked, but I knew the possibility had already been mooted. "I've had the scans, and they've only spotted one. No, it's just one enormous baby. Probably I'll have an eleven pounder. I'm praying for a caesarean: apart from anything else, I'd get a rest in hospital."

"Not a chance. All that beeping and muttering, and nurses shuffling round turning lights on when you least expect it, just so they can ask if you're having trouble sleeping. Then, when the baby arrives, they wake you up to tell you to go feed it. You might as well be here where your body can remember where the loo is, even when you can't get your eyes to open. Plus you'll have Jed here. He can put the baby on the boob without waking you up, and you can abuse him without having to worry it'll get written up in your notes."

"There speaks the voice of experience. Did you never think of having any more after Sam?"

Bernie was genuinely curious. It obviously hadn't occurred to her what pain she might be causing. That, more than anything, loosened the constraints I'd put on the subject. It was years since I'd thought about the events surrounding Sam's birth. Years. I tried to ignore the promptings of my memory: I'd been thinking about it that day in spring when I found the Calgary chess piece. But I hadn't allowed the train of thought to continue. It really was years since I had let myself touch on the detail, to go in beyond the memory of pain and the anguish of self-knowledge that had been forced on me afterwards.

"I…"

I couldn't speak for a moment. Sam's baby face swam up in front of me: his tiny, bruised form bristling with needles, tubes and monitoring equipment. I could feel again the deep nausea of my exhausted, depleted body, taking on the shock of seeing this, my precious first-born, for the first time. I had fainted then, and been carted back to the ward.

I don't even know how long it was until the next visit, perhaps days. Contrary to my cheerful assurances to Bernie, I don't know anything about getting up in the night to breast-feed my baby. By the time I had been well enough to begin to care for Sam, and he to have the stomach-feeding tube removed, my milk had dried up. I had been deprived of the chance to see him on his birth day, or even to touch him in his first few weeks, and had been so ill myself I was hardly aware of the lack.

By the time I came to be with him, we were strangers and had to learn one another all over again. It was something that could never be prepared for, and equally something I didn't want to talk about, least of all to someone anticipating the healthy birth of a normal baby. As if, by sharing my experience, I might somehow infect the other woman with its reality.

"Cas, I'm sorry. I didn't mean to upset you."

I realised tears were streaming down my cheeks. I scrubbed at them with my knuckles, and sniffed wetly. A small hand stuffed a grubby handkerchief into mine, and I gazed down into Tilly's concerned face. "It's all right, Tilly, I was just having a bit of a cry."

"I do 'at all da time," said Tilly, earnestly. "Shall I kissy better?"

"Yes, please." The exchange gave me the chance to get myself back under control. I turned to Bernie and grinned wanly.

"It's no good," she said. "You'll have to spill the beans."

She ushered Tilly out to her room and settled her with some biscuits broken into pieces for a dolls' picnic. I was grateful for the chance to compose myself, and readied myself to tell the tale when she returned and eased herself down onto the sofa again.

"I was seventeen when I married Drew. I fell pregnant almost straight away, but it was a difficult pregnancy. I felt morning sickness even before I missed my first period, and at the first antenatal check-up they were already concerned about my blood-pressure. Well, it continued to rise, and after the five-month check I was told that if it came up any further I would have to go into hospital for the rest of the pregnancy. It did – although I don't remember much about it. Just before my six-month check I collapsed while I was visiting my grandparents, and Nanna called an ambulance. By the time they got me to the hospital, I was already having convulsions. Eclampsia is the medical term for it: pathologically high blood pressure. It can kill the mother *and* the baby.

"Anyway, they got me stabilised and whipped Sam out by Caesarean. He was in a bad way: the functioning of the placenta had been compromised by the convulsions, and he needed oxygen. At three months premature he was a high risk baby, and they shipped him off immediately to the nearest paediatric intensive care unit with an available place, in Auckland. Over three hundred miles away.

"I was sent off a few days later; once I'd regained consciousness and they were fairly sure I'd live, they told me I could join him as soon as a bed became available. That was one of the less pleasant journeys of my life, but I consoled myself in lucid moments that I'd soon be holding my son. The reality was different: it was two weeks before I was allowed to slip a finger into the incubator and tuck it into his fist. I didn't hold him until he was four weeks old."

"Oh, Cas. You must have been heartbroken."

"I guess I was, but I didn't feel it for a long time. I was very weak despite blood transfusions, and I still had to go through all the post-birth experience of womb-contractions and bleeding. The trouble was, I didn't stop bleeding. I kept haemorrhaging, until they went back in for a second look. By that time I was prepared to agree to anything to make it stop, and when I came round they told me they'd had to perform a hysterectomy. Basically, my womb had begun to disintegrate and they couldn't save it. They told me that even if they could have repaired it, I would never have been able to carry another child. I think that was supposed to be comforting.

"I didn't feel the loss. I spent years on anti-depressants, learning to be a one-child woman, telling myself how lucky I was next to all the women who can't have children, or the ones who don't survive their first. And of course I put all my love into Sam: he's never had to deal with sibling rivalry, or neglect. There's always a silver lining," I finished.

By this time, Bernie was crying as well. She gulped back the tears and blew her nose loudly on a tea towel. She looked at it in surprise. "Oh, crap." Embarrassed, she stuffed it under a cushion. I giggled feebly as Bernie hauled herself to her feet. "Oh well, it was probably due a wash. Come and help me make another cuppa."

I dried a few dishes and amused myself guessing which cupboards they might belong to. Bernie's kitchen plan was a bit disorganised, to say the least. Then we carried our mugs outside to keep an eye on Tilly. I felt light-headed and happy; after sixteen years, the dreaded moment had come and I had talked about my experience. It hadn't killed me, and it didn't seem to have harmed Bernie.

For the first time I admitted to myself that there might have been value in talking about it before. Never mind: things happen when we need them to, and wishing can't alter the past. Bernie came past and gave me a sloppy hug, leaning forward over the bump, and I felt my heart open. "Thanks," I said.

"That's what friends are for. Now I know I can tell you all the gory details when Tiny arrives, and you won't have an excuse to stop me."

We collapsed onto the lawn, liberally spotted with daisies, and Bernie began making a daisy chain. This grassed area was her one garden luxury. Fully fenced to keep off the sheep, it had to be mown weekly in the summer, and Jed grumbled about it every time. Apart from the walled garden, and some large clumps of seemingly sheep-proof rhubarb, the house was surrounded by paddocks. The sheep and a small herd of Highland cattle took precedence over gardening. Bernie finished the daisy chain and slung it over Tilly's head. The recipient promptly went into royal mode, and began prancing round the garden, declaiming "I'm da queen. Listen to me, evvyone."

I glanced over at Bernie, and came under her clear and direct gaze.

"You talk about your grandparents," she said, "but you never mention your Mum and Dad. Is there a story there, too?"

"You really are digging out the skeletons," I said, secretly relieved not to be grilled any more about The Birth.

"My Mum was Nanna and Granddad's daughter. She died giving birth to me, and I've never known exactly why. Ever since Sam, I've wondered if she had the same problem I had, but even Nanna doesn't know. My Dad came from a nearby farm, but when he grew up he went into the army; he and Mum went to live on the army base at Waiouru. He'd already been posted to Vietnam when my Mum found out she was pregnant, and he didn't make it back. Nanna and Granddad made an epic journey to collect me from the hospital at Waiouru and bring me home. I'm not sure Granddad had ever been on the inter-island ferry before that."

I grinned, remembering. "Granddad used to tease me that he nearly dropped me over the side in a gust of wind. He reckoned I was a tiny scrap: weighed no more than a bit of thistledown. So I never knew either of my parents. Nanna had one black and white photo of Dad in his army uniform, and I used to sneak into her room and hold it up next to my face in the mirror, trying to see if I looked like him. I've often wondered if Sam inherited his grey eyes from my Dad, but I guess I'll never know. I don't know anything about his family, either.

"Nanna and Granddad brought me up. I lived with them until the day I married: straight out of school. I met Drew at a local dance. He'd just graduated from uni, and had been travelling around the world before starting work in the New Zealand branch of his father's firm. He was like no-one I'd ever met before: good-looking, charming, fun to be with. I was delirious with love, or with something anyway, and he carried me off to a life of riches and idleness."

I glanced over at Bernie. She'd met Drew, and had her own opinion of him which, generously, she'd kept to herself until after the divorce. She'd supported me without question, but I knew she believed I made the right decision in leaving him.

"Looking back, I can't imagine what I saw in him. By the time I recovered from Sam's birth and came back to him, we had nothing in common and barely a courteous word to say to each other. He made it clear he didn't want to be near me physically, although I don't know whether he resented the baby, hated that I'd become sickly and pale, or didn't like the fact that for a long while I was miserable all the time. He'd married me because I was fun to be with – when that stopped, he just couldn't be bothered.

"He kept me on as the trophy wife, safe and quiet at home, while he got on with all the high-flying business stuff he enjoys. There have been plenty of pictures of him with beautiful women on his arm, but at least he didn't bring any of them home with him. When he inherited the business, a few years later, we went with him to England.

"Nanna and Granddad never said a word; just loved and supported me, and picked up the pieces whenever it all went wrong. I used Drew's money, with no hesitation, to take us back there whenever I could get Sam away - every Christmas, if I could. I used to get into rows with Drew if Sam missed some school. The times I spent there, growing up, and later with Sam, were the best times of my life. I tried to pack them full of all the experiences I wanted Sam to have, knowing that once he went back to school I might not seen him for months.

"I was right to break with Drew. But I really miss being able to fly over and visit the farm and my Nanna and Granddad."

12

With the warm offshore wind behind me, I jogged back down towards the coast. I'd always intended to call in as I passed Bernie's house, but I'd ended up spending so long there that I no longer had time to run the long route via Torloisk, so I simply turned back the way I'd come that morning. I felt light of heart, but there was a strange, formless tension behind my eyes, as if at any moment my head was going to start aching. My heartbeat began to thud in my ears as I ran on. I gritted my teeth and picked up the pace.

By the time I arrived back at Calgary Bay I was perspiring furiously. At first glance, I could see that the day's crop of treasure hunters had gone. Two women were setting up tents in the small campsite at the western end of the bay, and Niall could be seen in the middle distance, addressing a large microphone, which was thrust into his face. As I stood, leaning against a tree trunk to catch my breath, I saw the reporter and his soundman draw away. I began a series of leg stretches, hoping my colour and heartbeat would have settled down before anyone noticed me. No chance. Sam came loping over.

"Hi Mum. Are you having a heart attack?"

"Oh, thanks. No. It's the effect of healthy exercise, if you must know. Not that you'd recognise the symptoms; you've probably spent the day lying on the beach catching rays."

"No way, Mum. We've really found something. Come and see." He dragged me off in the direction of a small knot of people. As we neared the group, Niall moved to join us, and I could hear the subdued sound of satisfied voices. Whatever they had found, they were pleased with it.

"Ah, Cas." Niall was uncharacteristically expansive. He

wrapped a warm arm round my damp shoulders, seeming oblivious to the aroma of sweat, and dragged Sam in under his other arm. I was astonished. Was this the same Mr Standoffish who had been lecturing me this morning? A man of many personalities, our Mr Webster.

The women from the campsite jogged over to join us as Niall began to explain: "Well, we have found something. But let's not go into it here. Bess and Maura are going to stay onsite tonight, in case we have any more visitors. The whole area of the machair has been searched with detecting equipment, and we're quite certain we've found what there is to find. Jay's team have already headed back to the ferry, so that leaves three of us to find food and accommodation. I suggest we repair to the pub for a meal, and then see if any rooms are available tonight."

I spoke up. "I can house all three of you for the night, so long as one of you doesn't mind a sofa-bed in the living room."

No objections were raised, and two tired archaeologists plodded off with their gear to the remaining Land Rover in the car park. Sam waved to Maura and Bess, and we left them to their lonely vigil. Niall spoke with them a moment, then jogged over to the Land Rover. He climbed in beside his mates and they headed off. Considering how tired everyone else looked, he was glowing with health and still seemed to have plenty of energy. Sam stood looking after them, but turned at my call and walked to the car, and we were away only a few minutes behind them.

I thought they might stop at the cottage to drop off their gear, which would give me the chance of a quick shower before a drink, but they headed straight for the village pub and piled in. By the time I'd parked and followed them in, a round of beers was on the table and the archaeologists were well into their first pints. "We've ordered fish and chips for everyone," announced a bearded man. "Hope you're all happy with that." He sat down to a chorus of "Cheers!", "Slainte!" and other such happy drinking terms. For a moment, the group could have been any gathering of drinkers, and then the talk began.

The bearded man introduced himself as Malcolm, trained as an archaeologist but, like many people in the Highlands and Islands, doing a completely different job to bring in an income. In his case it was driving trucks for the Forestry, which sent him all over the Highlands and gave him the opportunity for amateur archaeological research. He had taken leave to write up a paper on his last summer's research, but had been happy to drop everything when Niall called him.

The other man, younger and clean-shaven, was a teacher from Fort William. He and his wife ran a bed-and-breakfast in the season, but he had left her to cope alone when the chance of some real archaeology came up. They both knew the other archaeologists employed by AIAS, who were apparently all involved in a major dig on Islay. The reality of ferry travel in Western Scotland is that it would not have been possible for them to leave Islay and arrive on Mull within one day, so Niall had needed to look further afield for help.

There followed a vigorous discussion on the desirability of inter-island ferry links, as opposed to the existing situation where one had to travel backwards and forwards to the mainland in order to reach even the closest islands, making journeys long and expensive. This discussion dragged in several locals who had an interest, and degenerated into a general argument about politics. The food was long gone and the beer levels dropping for the fourth time when the little company regrouped and began to discuss the issue I cared about most: what had they found today?

Niall sat comfortably at the centre of attention. "We found something," he said. "Something really worthwhile. Unfortunately, we have not solved the origin of your mysterious chess piece. But we have found a cache."

"A what?" I asked, feeling ignorant.

"A cache is a deposit of material more-or-less unrelated to any other sign of archaeological activity in the area. So we haven't seen any evidence of settlement or other occupation sites in the machair at Calgary, but we have found one deposit of interesting artefacts. It's a small collection of objects: a ring brooch, and three coins. Preliminary study points to a date around 840-900AD. It's much too early to be related to your chessman, but it's very interesting nonetheless. No caches have ever been found in this part of Mull before."

"How do you know how old it is?"

"Malcolm, here, is our resident coins expert. Malcolm, would you…?"

The bearded forestry worker drained his pint, set down the glass and took up the tale. Niall slipped away from the table and went to the bar to order another round.

"We found three silver coins, and although two are rather battered and thin with no recognisable features, the third is less worn and resembles some coins known from Norway at this period. This doesn't mean they were deposited by a Norseman – no coins were being produced in Scotland in those days, so if people had any cash money it must have come from outside. The brooch is also of a style similar to Scandinavian examples dating from this period. The date is only a preliminary estimate, and will need to be confirmed officially, but I think we are looking at a cache from the late ninth century."

"Why do you think it was buried?" asked Sam. "Was it to keep it safe from Vikings?"

"Perhaps. It could have been put there by the local inhabitants, to keep it hidden from raiders. Other caches have been attributed to that purpose. If it had been a larger haul of coins, I would have thought it more likely to be Viking silver: either the results of a raid or a pay chest for mercenaries, buried to keep it safe until pay day. But with a very small deposit like this, there is another possible explanation."

We waited. Malcolm paused for effect, looking round to make sure he had everyone's attention, and then went on. "Small deposits may be ritual offerings. If Calgary was a sacred site, we might expect to find a number of such deposits. When there is only one, it may have been an offering for a specific purpose. For example, if a ship had been forced into Calgary Bay by bad weather, and the wind kept north-westerly for some time, they would not be able to leave.

"Ships of the time were not well designed for sailing to windward, and would not have been able to travel into a strong onshore wind. Here it's quite common for north-west winds to blow for many days at a time, especially during spring and autumn. Imagine a sailor, or perhaps the whole crew, contributing to an offering to the elements: giving up their own wealth to persuade the wind to drop and the sea to calm, so that they could leave safely."

We all fell silent for a moment. I remembered walking at Calgary during a westerly storm. I could well imagine how fierce the sea outside the bay must have been – probably I would have seen it, if I had cared to stare into a wind so strong that it dented the eyeballs. Even in the lee of the hills the waves can be fierce, and rocks line either side of the bay.

A modern sailing yacht with its efficient sailing arrangements, able to sail very close to the wind indeed, would still need to leave such an anchorage under power: using sail alone would be far too dangerous. Even with all its crew at the oars, a birlinn or a long ship would be terribly vulnerable to being thrust onto the rocks, or overturned in the surf. I thought about a band of raiders, or islanders caught on the wrong side of a battle between neighbours, desperate to leave shore and offering up their best and most precious possessions to persuade the weather to come round to their side and let them get away safely. I hoped they'd made it.

"But what about our queen?" My flight of imagination foundered on Sam's practicality. "What has that got to do with your cache?"

"Nothing. Absolutely nothing." Niall was back and adamant. "The cache is at least two hundred and fifty years too early to be related to our chess piece. Our chess queen seems to be contemporary with the Lewis pieces, and they fit well into the medieval period. Viking raids and internal squabbling had given way to extensive peacetime trading, and warfare occurred mainly between the forebears of the Lords of the Isles and other pretenders to power in the islands.

"Of course there were still raiding parties, but they were as often called pirates as Vikings, and they tended to raid wealthy places such as coastal towns and monasteries. If your piece came from such a raid, then we may never know its provenance. It could have lain hidden in the sands for centuries, as the Lewis pieces did. However much I would like to believe there are other pieces somewhere in the area, awaiting discovery, the evidence is against it. I think it's one of those finds that will remain an enigma, found out of context, and therefore of limited archaeological value, no matter how charming it is."

Niall's pronouncement seemed to dampen the spirits of the drinking party and, one by one, they rose and retrieved their coats. I led the Land Rover back to the cottage and found enough bedding for two more bodies: one on the truckle bed under Niall's in the spare room, and the other on the sofa. I handed over the blankets and sleeping bags and left them to it. I was mentally and physically exhausted, and wanted nothing more than to sink into my bed and sleep.

13

Saturday came in cold and miserable, quite a contrast to the last few days. I crawled out of bed late, to find the house deserted. When I shuffled downstairs in my dressing gown, I found a brief note thanking me for my hospitality. The archaeologists had left me £40, which I thought was kind of them, especially as they didn't seem to have eaten any breakfast. Three mugs were neatly stacked on the drainage board, but otherwise the kitchen was just as I'd left it.

I stuffed the money into the kitchen drawer and made a mental note to turn it into petrol as quickly as possible before the price went up again. There was no letter. No personal contact from Niall. No suggestion that I might ever find an excuse to see him again. Just as well. I wasn't interested. So there. I forbade myself to feel disappointment. I couldn't expect Niall Webster and his colleagues to keep loneliness from my door indefinitely, and my unexpected find in April had provided far more entertainment than I'd had any right to expect.

Sam was nowhere to be seen, and a quick peek into his room revealed his bedclothes and yesterday's clothes on the floor, but no boy. When I checked in the porch and discovered that his football gear had disappeared, I guessed he'd gone down to the village pitch to see if there was a game on. As soon as I thought the word football, I remembered the notice outside the village shop. Was today the inter-village footie tournament? Maybe. If so, then turnout might be lower than usual – they were no doubt hoping for better weather. I hoped he'd enjoy himself, and tried not to think about the muddy boots and extra laundry.

I glimpsed my sour-faced reflection in the window, shaken by a sudden gust of wind and distorted by drops flung at the pane. I sneezed, and then winced as the raw patch in the back of my throat smarted. All that sniffling yesterday had been more than just a reaction to exercise; I must have already been incubating this cold, and today it had decided to exert itself.

I went to the kitchen intending to make coffee and toast, but ended up with warm water and some painkillers. I made my way back to bed and tried to get comfortable, but every time I lay down my nose blocked and I couldn't breathe properly. Standing up was no better: a throbbing sinus headache was threatening and all my joints ached. Work, or even thinking about work, was definitely out of the question. I wedged myself half-upright in bed and tried not to think about anything.

For a while I attempted to meditate, and to persuade myself I felt better than I did, but my head was throbbing in time with my pulse and with my eyes shut I felt dizzy. So I gazed at nothing and let my thoughts ramble round my head, which seemed to work slightly better than trying to empty my mind altogether. The interminable morning wore on, but eventually the painkillers started to work and I perked up a bit.

A day spent in bed mollycoddling a cold is never wasted, despite a few guilt pangs about: money (work not done = no income); housework (half a tin of kitchen paint drying out in the porch); family (one moody, misunderstood adolescent son. I don't know what to do – I never even had a Mum); relationships (a gorgeous, intelligent man apparently wedded to his work, and another whose attractions are only now making themselves apparent to me, when he's already got used to me being just one of his mates); and so on. I wallowed in it, and pampered myself with a hot lemon-ginger drink and a little bit of my secret stash of chocolate. I knew I was starting to recover when I began to be able to taste the stuff.

Leaning back against the pillows I closed my aching eyes and allowed my mind to butterfly from one random thought to another. Gradually I sank into a dozy half awareness. Not quite able to fall completely into sleep, I remained peripherally aware of the warmth of my body. After years of training it to lie quiet, it was beginning to awaken. I learned early on in my marriage that physical arousal led to disappointment, and found I derived far more satisfaction from intellectual pursuits and in caring for my child.

Drew found intelligence in a woman unattractive, and frequently reminded me of the fact. I'd dealt with the loneliness of Sam's first few years at boarding school by enrolling at university, and poured all my energies into study. When I persisted in my coursework, Drew lost interest in my body altogether, which was a relief. He saved face, however, by claiming that my First Class Honours degree was proof standards were slipping and it must be becoming easier to obtain a degree. I didn't care; I was pursuing the life of the mind, and I liked to see myself as part of the great tradition of women who choose (or are lucky enough to be offered the choice) to learn.

Not that it was all about the life of the mind. There was one man in particular, one of the university librarians. A lovely man, both handsome and courteous, his hand had touched mine as he helped me balance a particularly heavy pile of texts. For the rest of the day I had carried round with me the electric memory of that touch, knowing nothing more would happen, but returning again and again to the pleasure of the contact. Then I met his wife: a redheaded post-graduate student, beautiful and ferociously intelligent. I felt small, pale and slow-witted beside her, and had crept gratefully back into my shell with only a small sigh of disappointment.

I don't think I've been attracted to anyone else from that day to this, and here I am drawn to two men at once. It must have something to do with the divorce. I'm no longer tied to someone who despises me, while still considering that he owns me body and soul. For the first time in my life I am an adult and answerable to no-one else. (Anything could happen. Next step skinny-dipping in winter, and then I take to the gin.)

I shifted about awkwardly in the bed, trying to get comfortable. There's no denying I feel attracted to Niall, but he has such a strange reserve about him. Monk-like, he seems to have set aside bodily demands and lives for his work alone. He appears to have no friends, no family, no relationships outside his work colleagues. Is he really so firmly attached to his work that there is no room in his life for anything other than archaeology? He must be no more than seven or eight years younger than me. He's obviously eligible. Why isn't he married? That beautiful golden body cries out to be caressed and loved. Still, unless I find another chess piece there's damn all chance I'll ever meet him again.

My thoughts turned to the other candidate in my small pool of fantasy objects: the enigmatic Ewan MacInnes. Despite my insistence that inviting him and his Dad to Christmas dinner had been a gesture of neighbourly friendliness (not to mention desperation, given Sam was hardly speaking to me at the time), I did find myself drawn to Ewan. His quiet voice, laconic manner and tall, fit body seemed ideally suited to his life on Mull: out on the sea in all weathers, escorting tourists or fishing.

Drew had hired him and his boat in a number of previous summers, and I'd always thought him so alive compared to other men – confident in himself, not needing anyone else's approval. But I knew little about him. That Christmas I had mostly conversed with Hector, when I wasn't busy in the kitchen, hearing his tales of times gone by. Lives spent working in the open air; dark, warm houses once filled with people and smoke, now roofless and abandoned. Village populations ever decreasing through death or emigration and then, during Hector's lifetime, a gradual increase in the number of incomers and a rise in the island's population again.

Ewan barely entered into these conversations and he

remained distant except when talking to Sam about the fishing and his new boat. I was very grateful for the attention shown to Sam, who had relaxed and expanded under its influence, becoming much easier to live with. But I had no real insight into the man himself: only his strong body presented itself to my mind's eye, and I ran my mental gaze over it. I toyed with a vague sense of arousal, warming my body and tweaking a frisson of lust, but I must have dozed off mid-contemplation, because I came to, feeling worse than ever, cradling my head in my hands and trying not to sneeze. I moaned as my sinuses throbbed and gave up on getting out of bed just yet.

Sam had arrived, and I could hear him banging and muttering his way around the kitchen. I didn't even want to guess what was bothering him this time; he seemed so happy yesterday. Eventually he slammed his way into upstairs and into my room.

"What's for dinner?" he demanded.

I don't know what I looked like, but he backed straight out again, turning up a few minutes later with a cup of tea for me.

"Mum, are you okay? You look terrible."

"Thank you very much." I laughed, but immediately regretted it, as it made my throat hurt.

"What about a hot water bottle? Can I make you some soup? Do you want a back rub?" Sam plonked himself down on the edge of the bed, ready to think up other supportive suggestions.

"No thanks. The tea's perfect – just what I needed."

"Are you sure? I don't mind making you some dinner."

"I really don't want anything. You could have the leftover curry in the fridge, though. Cook yourself some rice, and there's a pack of naan bread in the freezer. Would you turn on the boiler while you're down there? From the amount of mud I can see from here, I guess you need a bath."

Despite my refusal, Sam did bring up a hot water bottle and a mug of soup, although he didn't stay to keep me company. After a huge plate of curry, followed by a great deal of splashing and wallowing, the adolescent hippopotamus hauled itself out of its water hole and collapsed into bed with half a malt loaf and two new DVDs. Bless.

After sleep, Sam's soup and most of a medieval murder mystery, I felt much better, and resolved to put the whole Calgary chess piece episode behind me. If the weather improved, we would go fishing on Monday with Ewan, and I wanted to concentrate on getting well in time for that. It might prove a chance to reach Sam – to try and understand his lightning changes of mood.

I didn't remember being anything like as volatile when I was a teenager, although I suspect if I asked Nanna and Granddad I might be told a few things I didn't want to hear. I leaned back on my pillows and promised myself I would practise patience, tolerance and forbearance. I was so pleased with my resolutions that I crawled out of my sickbed and spent two hours on Henry's new assignment: a dry and difficult Chemistry text, thankfully only sparsely scattered with proofreading errors.

As I worked, my nose began to run again and the headache slowly worsened. A little is better than nothing, and I had to admit I'd reached my limit for today. In the end, I crept into the bathroom and, closing the door tightly with a wedge of flannel, ran the bath and started to breathe in the steamy atmosphere.

I lay back in the bath sucking a lemon-oil cough drop and trying to ignore my aching sinuses, groaning contentedly as the hot water wrapped around my back and lapped my chilled shoulders. In a cloud of steam I relaxed at last. Forget the wind coughing down the chimney, the flurries of rain and the unseasonal cold. Time to visit my favourite place in all the world: my secret paradise, Huna Cove. With a sigh of pleasure, I leaned back and closed my eyes.

The hammer of sun beat down on my face, my closed eyelids red with the brightness of it. I could feel the crisp hardness of sand: cool under my body where I had absorbed its heat; hot under my searching hands. The gritty roughness of it ran between my fingers: tiny rounded particles clinging to my skin. I rubbed my palm over my thigh and felt its sandpapery texture. As I breathed I could smell brine, and a fresh herby smell, from the fitful breeze that came to me across lush lowland rainforest vegetation and piles of sun-heated seaweed. I ran my tongue over my lips and tasted a thin layer of salt. I stood up and opened my eyes.

At first blinded by the sun striking molten silver off the sea, I could see nothing but the shocking turquoise of the water. As my sight cleared, I looked around. Ahead, the warm sand edged away into a sparkling sea. The sun stood high in the vault of the sky and bathed me with its beneficent glow.

I turned a full circle, taking in the tiny crescent of beach, backed by a small cliff, itself topped with a green tapestry of leaf, fern and creeper; a verdant brocade spilling over the cliff and weaving itself over every surface. At the foot of the cliff, a tiny creek emerged from a green pool, filled by the constant curtain of drops spilling down the cliff face. The streamlet meandered away across the sand to enter the sea at the northern end of the beach. There the cliff edge reached the water, and in places the streamlet diverted into deep, green undercut pools. Around these, a damp shaded coolness prevailed, redolent of herbs and earth and moist stone. To my right the cliff fell away into a tumble of rocks and briny pools, which would be covered at high tide, but presently stretched away into the ocean, like some tumbled causeway of immeasurable antiquity.

Coming full-circle, I gazed back into the blue immensity of the southern ocean. The horizon was a shimmering insubstantiality, imperceptibly merging sea and sky. Right at the edge of sight I glimpsed a brief flicker of light, or whiteness – perhaps a whale spouting, before submerging again on its ancient migratory sea-path.

I sat back onto my heels and, digging my fingers into the sand, examined the handful I was sifting. Although most of the grains were yellow sandstone, I could see there were also tiny red flakes of garnet, white quartz, the charcoal-coloured, indurated sandstone called greywacke, some black crumbs of basalt: every grain millennia old, each stolen by the sea from the bones of the earth, ground and polished to this coarse powder. Even a few grains of milky green, like precious specks of pounamu. I rasped my hands together to shake off the loose grains, and then lay back on a warm patch. I rubbed my nose where it itched. Under the brazen heat of the sun, the distant susurration of the sea was an irresistible lullaby.

Slowly, I drifted away.

I snorted and sat up quickly, coughing the water from my mouth. It tasted unpleasantly soapy. The bath water was tepid and scummy.

"Damn," I muttered aloud.

Falling asleep in the bath is no solution to the miseries of a cold. I dried my face and rubbed my sore nose on the hand towel, then tossed it into the laundry basket. Stepping out of the bath, I wrapped myself in a bath towel that would have been warm if it hadn't slipped off the towel rail during my doze. My nose still itched, and grumpy sinuses promised more headache. Time for pills and sleep, and let the morning shed a fresh light on anything left undone today. I pulled out the plug and headed for bed.

In my dreams that night, I came again to Huna Cove. As I scuffed across the sand, my foot snagged an object. I groped for it with my fingers and found I was grasping the Calgary queen. As I placed it on my outstretched palm, its gnome face blinked and scowled. Then the little queen stood up, turned her throne about and sat down with her back to me.

I shivered. Suddenly a biting wind arose, whipping my nightdress against my bare legs. Sand picked up by the wind stung my skin. Ahead of me, the sun was going down in a blood-red haze. The sea sucked at the sand under my feet as I fought to keep my balance. There was no stable surface.

14

I sat back in the bottom of the boat and trailed a hand over the side: a ripple of water cool as silk caressed my fingers. Thirty-six hours of real work and decent sleep had put the cold behind me, and only the last remnants of it tickled my throat and made me cough occasionally. Sam and I had risen early that morning, breakfasted rapidly and amicably, then grabbed our coats and drinks and made for Croig harbour, on the north coast. I love Croig. It's always quiet and laid-back, and the tiny harbour is seldom stirred by waves even when the north wind is beating on the coast outside the pier. The old boat hulk slowly disintegrating on the harbour bottom, exposed at low tide and gradually collapsing under its own weight, provides a powerful message about the fate of all objects which have ceased to be useful. Ewan's own boat, *Martha-Margaret*, lies in the deeper channel, securely moored, its lovingly polished lineaments promising it will never suffer the fate of its rusted neighbour.

Croig was once the cattle-landing point for islands to the north and west, and for the communities of the Ardnamurchan peninsula – that lonely and forlorn-looking mainland terrain, even more isolated than Mull. In those days the harbour must have rung to the shouts of drovers, the moaning of cattle and the crying of gulls overhead.

The old droving inn is still there, and offers self-catering accommodation to tourists, but those who stay find barely an echo of the old busyness of the cattle drive. There's a small local fishing industry operating from the pier, as there must always have been, but otherwise walkers, and the occasional wildlife tour vehicle, are the only visitors.

Sam was quiet too. After a sustained and lively discussion

103

with Ewan about why we were not going out on the big boat (too expensive, and not so much fun on a calm day) he had settled down in the bow of *Faoileag* and set up his line carefully, following Ewan's guidance.

The last time Ewan had taken us out was with Drew, in our last summer together. We'd gone out on *Martha-Margaret*. I thought at the time that it was simply a question of money: Drew paid for the big boat, so Drew got the big boat. But I was having so much fun fishing from the smaller vessel (and finding it easier to haul up the occasional fish I did catch) that I suspected Ewan must have known he wasn't giving us the best option back then. Perhaps it was a local's revenge on the rich tourist who thought he knew better: give him what he expects. No more. No less. No doubt the twelve foot sailing sloop, with her mast stepped and the outboard motor installed, was a cheaper proposition for three sailors, but I also appreciated Ewan sharing his own boat with us.

A tug on the line recalled me to the present. I drew it up swiftly, only to see a silver shape flash back into the green-blue depths. Ewan's deep laugh sounded briefly at my shoulder. "Don't be so impatient. Draw it up slowly, now. Mackerel are easy fish – they want to be caught."

He proved his point by carefully raising his own line, each of the three hooks adorned by a still-wriggling fish. He gently eased each fish from the hook, and let the line back down. "On a good day you don't even need bait; they take the bare hook. My Grandfather used to say the mackerel must be Christian fish, because if you said the blessing before you went out, they would jump into your boat willingly, just for the opportunity to feed Christian souls."

"Your Grandfather? Was that Hector's father?" Hector MacInnes had been left at home with the dog, being unenthusiastic these days about the romance of fishing. He had promised himself a walk to the pub in the afternoon, for a drink and a smoke with old friends who still called him

Eochainn, and would chat in the Gaelic. He had, however, insisted he would be home in time for his mackerel supper.

"No, that was my Mum's Dad, Ruairidh MacLean. He lived in the old village at Haunn, in Treshnish. Most of the people left there during the smallpox epidemic. Some went to the poorhouse in Tobermory, but many went to the mainland or away overseas. The land went over to sheep, after that. Grandda's folk were allowed to stay for some reason. They had a croft right down on the shore, and they always did a bit of fishing. He said the other people in the village had their eyes turned away from the sea, except for the kelp-harvesting, and that even the famines of the clearance years couldn't make fishermen out of farmers.

"Myself, I think that was a bit arrogant. Without good gear and knowledge, you can't get much, and I never heard that anyone in the village but Grandda really knew how to care for the nets and the boat.

"Ruairidh and his wife lived a pretty isolated existence. Every now and then, he'd take some fish up to the houses inland, and trade for whatever they needed at home. I think the travellers used to come round too, in the summer – it's a nice place to stay, till you get moved on. They had just the one daughter, Ealasaid, and she ran off and married my Dad first chance she got. So she used to tell me anyway. She could never understand why I wanted to be going down to that dreich old place, but I loved it. As soon as school was out for the summer I was down there, barefoot on the stones, helping my Grandda with the nets."

This was the longest speech I'd ever heard from Ewan. I didn't want to move and break the spell. I'd never been to Haunn, but I knew the old schoolhouse at Reudle, which had served all the little villages and communities in the area. Its grim three-storey bulk is set in a bleak landscape of moor and rock, exposed to all weathers. I'd heard the story of the children who, walking miles to school each day, had to each carry a peat to heat the school when they got there. For the teacher, living alone in the top storey, it must have been a dreary and lonely existence.

"Did your Mum go to Reudle School?" I asked. Ewan shrugged.

"No," he said. "I guess she would have been at school in the 1920s, but the school at Reudle was long closed by then. There used to be a rule that primary children had to have a minimum of one-hundred attendances a year, with each morning or afternoon counting as one. So every winter her Mam moved with her into Mornish, and they stayed with friends so she could go to the Mornish school. My mother remembered it as a horrible time: they were really in service, working all the time to pay their keep, and school was the only nice thing about it. Except that she met my Dad there.

"She used to say she missed school all the summer and autumn, when she was the only child on the croft, and then all winter she would miss her Dad and the peace of the coast. But once she married she hardly went back, only when old Ruairidh died and she had to care for her Mam. Gran only outlasted Grandda by a few weeks. After that, the croft fell empty, and no-one has lived there since."

I thought of the little family, subsisting alone in such an isolated place. I tried to imagine what that stretch of coast must be like: rough and exposed in places, backed by the great basalt terraces of the north Mull trap country. In my mind's eye I saw a tiny indentation in the black cliffs, a patch of sand and rough grass with a solitary blackhouse, dark and low, its thatch held down by a network of ropes and hanging stones. What would it be like to live in such an environment: beauty and hardship mixed, with the same unchanging tasks to be performed day after long summer day?

Sam and Ewan were laughing. I glanced across to see that they were trying to clear a disastrous tangle in Sam's line, but that wasn't the cause of the laughter. Sam was telling Ewan about our archaeological mystery.

"I heard about that," said Ewan. "You had half the population of Argyll over with their metal detectors, hoping to make their fortune, and all to show for it was a few coins and a bit of bone."

"Ivory!" retorted Sam.

"Walrus ivory, only. I think your archaeological comrades were hoping for the treasure of Troy, the amount of equipment they brought with them."

"They did a proper investigation and were very happy with the result," I said primly.

"Well…"

A long silence ensued, while Ewan fought with the last tangles in the line. At last he raised his eyes again. "Did they say anything about the find my grandfather made, off the north coast here?"

"No." Sam was excited, and I sat up and paid attention again. "What was it?"

"Grandda and his mate were fishing when they found they were caught up on the bottom. They got the net free after a bit, and hauled it to check the damage. When they brought it in, there was something caught in the mesh: a bit of twisted metal. They nearly threw it back in, but something made Grandda look a bit closer, and he saw there was a design etched into a flat part of the metal.

"He took it home and cleaned it up, and it still looked like a bit of nothing, but it was a nothing that someone had taken the trouble to carve with a design. There were some curved lines, and an animal like a wolf or a dog, he said. Anyway, eventually my Dad took it into Tobermory to show it to a man who was visiting there, and he thought it was important and took it off to Edinburgh, to put in the museum."

He paused and scanned the horizon, then started the motor and moved the boat a few hundred yards along the shoreline. He lowered his line overboard and sat silently, watching the glint of sunlight on the water. I realised he hadn't dropped anchor and wondered how safe that was. I gazed inland for a few minutes and realised we were drifting almost imperceptibly along the shoreline. But the rate of movement was so slight that it would probably take hours to get into really shallow water. I decided to stop worrying, and let my own line down into the water. I was used to these long silences of Ewan's, and waited patiently for him to take up the story again, but Sam had no such reserve. "What was it?" he asked.

"They said it was part of a set of scales. Very small scales, for measuring small weights. Maybe belonging to a trader whose boat sank in these parts. It didn't look like much, according to Grandda. He reckoned they could have said it was anything, and you'd just have to believe them or not, as you chose. They did say it was probably early medieval in date, though. Something about the style of the engraving. Anyway," he went on, "I think we have enough fish for today. Haul in, Cas, and we'll go for lunch."

I obediently hauled away, and was rewarded with the last catch of the day. I dropped it into the bucket and sat back as Ewan steered the boat around the headland. He turned south-west into a small, calm bay and tossed out anchor in only two feet of water. He and Sam slipped over the side and made her fast fore and aft to a pair of rocks on shore.

Then Ewan waded back out and hoisted me, picnic basket and all, and carried me in to shore. Sam was laughing at the sight of me, dwarfed by the basket with my legs sticking up in the air, and I got the giggles too. So much so that Ewan almost dropped me. I glared darkly at the two laughing men, then shrugged and brushed the sand from my trousers. Feeding the animals would settle them down.

After a good meal supplemented by a welcome tot of whisky from Ewan's hip-flask, I lay back and gazed at the sky. A thin haze of cloud still covered the sun, but the tiny bay was sheltered and warm. Ewan was showing Sam how to catch flatfish, down in the shallows, and I could hear giggles whenever my son almost stood on one of the little fish, which are almost invisible under a thin covering of sand until they suddenly move. Without a spear or net, success was bound to be elusive, and when the two gave up and sat themselves down on the sand beside me, Sam put on his best imitation of Ewan's accent and claimed that all the fish in this bay were "just bairns, too small to be worth the catching."

Sam lay on his back, gazing up into the thinning haze. He covered his eyes with his arm and relaxed. I rolled to one side and looked over his body towards Ewan, propped up on one arm as he gazed out to sea. I ran my eyes over his strong, lean form, seeing how his hair was lightened and his skin darkened in places by exposure to the sun. The sleeves of his faded, cotton shirt were rolled to above the elbow and I could see a puckered scar on one forearm, the kind of scar that might result from a barbed fishhook being dug out of the skin. Looking at him, I could sense in my fingertips how the rough skin of the scar would feel, and the smoothness of the warm flesh next to it.

I wondered at this man, whom I had met as my husband's employee, but who had become a friend in that long, lonely first winter on Mull when I was husbandless, jobless and to all intents and purposes childless, apart from the school holidays. The first few times I had run into him, out walking the dog, I had fallen in beside him and kept him company for a little while. Even then I already felt comfortable in his silent presence, and responded to his invitations to come in and spend time with Hector. (Generally all he did was jerk his head toward the house and look at me, but I knew what he meant.)

I already felt at home with Hector, and quickly fell into the habit of calling on him, and taking the dog for a walk if Ewan was away. I have become very fond of Hector and Molly, and enjoy the elderly man's conversational reminiscences. Many a time if I feel the need of company and I've missed my daily chat with the postie, I run round to Hector's for tea and a talk. More often than not Ewan is away working. He may not even know how often I spend an afternoon with his Dad.

If Ewan is home, he walks me back with Molly. The three of us have walked, and run, many miles in company, and I've come to see the man as just another silent animal companion, like the dog, in whose presence I have nothing to prove. It's pleasant to spend time with someone who expects nothing from you.

All that time Ewan had remained an enigma. Today, at last, I had been shown a glimpse of the man behind the guarded exterior, and I was intrigued. As I mused, my eyes still on his profile, Ewan turned and met my gaze. His face remained expressionless, but he held my eyes for a long, measuring moment. Then he smiled, and that changed his face completely. I responded instantly to the light in his eyes, and smiled myself, but in the same instance I flushed and dropped my gaze. When I looked up again he was getting to his feet. "Time is getting on," he said.

By the time we'd loaded up and manoeuvred the little boat out onto open water, the afternoon was fast slipping away. Ewan took us straight back to Croig; the slight wind that had come up turned the water choppy, but the powerful outboard motor made nothing of it. Back at the croft, we piled out with our bucket of fish to see Hector being helped out of the passenger seat of an old Bedford truck. His companion was Jed Kavanagh. Hector was clearly a little the worse for wear, and he clutched at Jed's arm to get his balance.

"Congratulations, man," he said, then turned and made his unsteady way toward the kitchen door. Behind him, Molly jumped carefully down from the cab and followed her master into the house. I looked expectantly at Jed.

"Tiny has arrived," he said, "and is now Emma Jane, nine pounds two ounces, mother and baby doing well."

"Congratulations," we all said together, and Ewan shook Jed's hand and brought out his hip flask.

"Oh no," Jed demurred. "I've already had my fair share down at the pub. Hector would never have let me away without drinking one celebratory dram. But I'm away to collect Tom and Tilly from their Nan, and it wouldn't do to be drinking and driving." Mrs Neville, Bernie's Mum, was a famous teetotaller and more frightening than the forces of the law.

"Was it quick?" I asked, wondering if Bernie had tried to contact me. I hoped she hadn't needed me – when I agreed to go over and be with her during the birth I assumed I would only be a phone call away.

"Yep. Easy as an old ewe dropping a lamb."

Ignoring this piece of farmer's wisdom, I asked Jed to pass on my love to Bernie.

"Come over and see her," he said. "She'd love to see you."

"Here," Sam was holding out a packet of peppermints. "Have one of these. It will freshen your breath."

"Don't mind if I do. Anything to keep the old bat from noticing I've had a drink."

"That was the idea." Sam grinned as he returned the mints to his pocket.

I looked askance at that. What did Sam know of the need to disguise the smell of drink? Indeed, what exactly did he get up to at school when he wasn't chained to a desk? I had visions of beer drinking sessions in some dark corner of the school (behind the bike sheds it was in my school) following by frantic sucking of mints to cover up the smell.

I remembered my reluctant year of prefect duty, sent to catch smokers round the back of the History prefab, under orders to report the names of rule-breakers to the Deputy Head. I taught myself to whistle. The wheezy sounds of my approach would lead to giggling and whispering, and scrabbling noises. By the time I rounded the corner, I would find nothing but a cloud of foul smelling smoke. I had the lowest rate of 'capture' of any prefect, and the teachers soon learned there wasn't any point in sending me out after smokers.

Don't get me wrong: I think smoking is a foul habit. But compared to some of the really bad stuff that went on at school (bullying for instance) I couldn't bring myself to care about the idiots who smoked. The only people they were harming were themselves. I regarded Sam with suspicion, but told myself not to be so paranoid.

Jed took off in a cloud of dust and fumes and we retreated to the house, where Hector had the kettle on and four mugs ready for the tea. I settled to the fireside, where I chatted with Hector, while Ewan lectured Sam on the esoterica of cleaning, gutting and cooking mackerel. The meal, when it did come, was delectable. Fish so fresh and moist that it fell off the bones and melted in our mouths. Thick slabs of buttered bread from the bakery in Tobermory, delivered that morning by van to households all over the island, and more tea, dark and strong with plenty of milk. With an apple each to finish, it was a meal fit for paradise, and we all ate far too much. Ewan lay back in an old armchair and stretched out his long legs, and Sam threw himself down on the rug in front of the fire.

Just as we were all getting warm and sleepy, Sam's phone rang. He got up and shuffled out to the hallway with it clamped to his ear. As he left the room he said, "Yeah…hi Dad," and my heart sank. I knew what that was about. Last summer holiday we were in the middle of the separation process, and Drew tried constantly to persuade Sam to go away with him. Sam wouldn't go; convinced that if he left me alone in the 'family' home I would leave. Quite possibly he was right. He clung to me, and refused to go anywhere without me, which infuriated Drew.

By Christmas, I was well settled on Mull and once Sam had seen I was okay he agreed to spend the last week of the holiday with Drew, who had then delivered him back to school on time as promised. That had been the Christmas of the evil temper and ominous silences, though, and I had considered that the prospect of a week with Drew might be one of the causes of those.

I don't know how much contact Sam has with his Dad during term time, but it can't be much. Last week's phone call was all about trying to set up a last-minute 'holiday' with Sam – as if a week of intensive Daddying can make up for the absence of any regular fathering.

Sure enough, Sam returned looking sheepish. "Mum," he said in persuasive tones, "Dad wants me to go away with him. The boat's ready, and he's setting off tomorrow. He's going to pick me up in Oban at four o'clock." His eyes pleaded with me, willing me not to make difficulties in front of other people.

"Of course," I said.

Sam grinned in relief. "Can we go home and pack?"

We made our apologies and departed the MacInnes home, leaving the hearthside to Molly and Hector. Ewan walked with us as far as the gate and then turned aside to his own caravan in the paddock next door. He eats most of his meals in the house with his Dad, but prefers the privacy of his own space otherwise. The caravan was plenty big enough, he said.

He held out his hand to Sam, who shook it. "I'll be in touch about that other matter."

Sam nodded. "I'll look forward to that."

I wondered what Sam was planning, but reined in my curiosity for the sake of peace, and we made our way home in the never-quite-dark of the late summer evening, trying to dodge the midges and laughing as we failed miserably.

15

I drove Sam to the ferry terminal at Craignure on Tuesday morning. He shrugged his backpack onto his shoulders and I watched him walk off without a backwards glance. As his tall, slender form made its way down the long glass tunnel toward the ferry entrance my perspective suddenly shifted, so that I saw not a nearly-grown adult but a small boy, dwarfed by his backpack, heading off to school. The memory shocked me with its immediacy – another moment I had buried, and hoped not to have to think about again.

Sam had been desperately afraid of school, and had clung to me, pleading with me not to make him go. It had been desperately difficult to hide from him my own fear and anger at the forced separation. I told him, over and over again, that it would be okay and that I would see him again in the holidays, until at last he agreed to go. My last sight had been that small figure, dwarfed by his school bag, walking towards the car, and then his white face in the window as Drew pulled away. I'd been upstairs, staring through the bedroom window. I banged on the glass, but he couldn't hear me. He left believing I had chosen to let him go without saying goodbye.

I couldn't bear to imagine how lonely and strange he must have felt for those first few weeks, waiting and waiting to go home, until he finally accepted that it wasn't going to happen. I didn't see him again until half-term break. Drew went down to collect him. He made it clear that I was not to go near the school and, when I protested, he told me there were suitable schools all over the world and no need for Sam to attend one in the same country I was living in.

As soon as I saw him again, I could see he had grown; taller, thinner; and paler I thought, although that might have been just the loss of his summer colour. More than anything, though, he was reserved. When prompted he came forward and kissed me, said "Hello," then he followed his father. It was like having a polite changeling in the house. It took a couple of days, once Drew was back at work, for his reserve to thaw, but even then he wouldn't talk about school. When I asked him directly, "What happened at school this term?" he would always say, "Oh, nothing."

Once I told him I would be coming to his parent/teacher evening and I was sure his teachers would tell me all the things he got up to. He pulled away from me immediately and ran for his pencils and paper. He wrote out a complete timetable of a week's classes, and what they had been studying in each, so that I wouldn't need to go to school and meet his teachers. I never told him Drew would not have allowed me to go.

I don't think anything really bad happened to him at school. All three of the places attended (two in New Zealand, and now the Scottish school) had very good reputations and Sam learned a lot. But one of the things he learned was a strong, independent reserve.

Whenever faced with any indefinable and vaguely threatening situation, Sam will square his shoulders in the same way he did at five years old, and stride straight forward to meet his fear. Today it made me wonder what it was he feared in his upcoming meeting with his father, but it did no good to worry. If I knew one thing about Sam, it was that he would keep his problems to himself until he was ready to share them.

Even in the turbulent years of adolescence, and the misery of his parents' break-up, he kept that core of inner calm intact. Until last year at least. I wondered what in particular had set off his volatile outbursts over the last few months. I'd give a lot to know if his behaviour had changed at school, or only when he was 'safe' with me?

I envied him that powerful private persona: a place deep

within that no-one can touch. What unmet need could have triggered such a thing? Did Sam's fear of the unpredictable, and his reserved and hidden self trace back to his traumatic birth, and the weeks spent in isolation, hardly touched from one day to the next? I didn't regret my failure to have more children (I don't. I won't!), but I would have given almost anything to have carried that child under my heart for a few more weeks. To have given him the gift of normal birth, and to have held him skin-on-skin from the very beginning of his independent life is the deepest wish of my heart, an impossible wish. For better or worse, Sam's life began in pain, fear and loneliness, and not all the mother-love in the world can undo that.

Sam had long since gone, and the ferry's bow door was closing as it pulled away from the link span. There was no point in searching deep into the past to understand Sam's behaviour. For all I knew he was having the same problems dealing with his father that he had with me. I almost felt sympathy with Drew – did he know what he was letting himself in for, taking the teenager from hell away on holiday? I rubbed my temples with a sigh and turned away. Time to get my head down: a week on my own would enable me to finish the job for Henry, and that meant payment, which was not to be sneezed at.

Four days of concerted effort saw off the wretched Chemistry textbook, and I sent the results to Henry, along with a note that I needed a change, and would he please send me some New Age poetry to proofread? After that I set about cleaning the house from top to bottom, starting with the computer desk, which had got horribly dusty while we'd been busy with archaeological capers.

I missed the little queen, whose pleasant scowl had kept me company for so many months, but I'd managed to pick up a plastic model of a warder, the rook piece from the Lewis Chessmen, in the ferry gift shop. This one wasn't a berserker, just a wee bloke with a shield. He didn't have the same ferocious charm as my grumpy queen. I put the little man back down on the desk, but my eye was drawn back to him. I kept telling myself I had to let the whole thing go, but something was still brewing in the back of my mind – something. "Let it be," I told myself. "It will come out when it's ready".

'Dear Cassandra,

Thank you. Sterling work as usual. You are my most reliable employee – most people seem to think that deadlines are some kind of optional extra.

Marise is well. As you know, she's gone up to Oxford to study Pol Sci and Law. She's already letting the side down though. She's got herself a man, and, unbelievably, he's a policeman. The idea is terrifying. Not that I would ever break the law, I'm far too frightened of the consequences, but I'm still horrified. I thought she'd find a nice barrister, or a Professor of Divinity. Someone to keep her in style when the old fart kicks the bucket.

I'm sorry you found the Chemistry text so dry. Can't imagine why you'd have that response. How about I send you something new? I have the latest draft of 'The Young Person's Guide to Quantum Mechanics in a Relativistic Universe.' How's that for New Age?

Love to the boy. I hope he's behaving himself. Do come and visit the next time you're down this way. I'll take you out and show you all the things you're missing, living in the back of beyond.

All my love,

Henry.'

I giggled. "Idiot," I said. I wondered idly if there was such a volume as the *YPG to QM* etcetera. It sounded horrifyingly plausible. At the end of the vacuuming, as I shifted the furniture back into place, I found myself wondering if I ought to clean the windows.

"Time for a walk," I said aloud. Cas Longmore rule of thumb: except in early spring, when the sun streams through the glass for the first time in four months and shows up horrific levels of dirt, thinking about cleaning the windows always means you've got too obsessive about housework. Turning my back on the whole housekeeping thing, I snatched up my fleece and pulled on my old running shoes.

I set off along the road without a backwards glance, putting as much space as possible between myself and all the serious realities of life. A long, tiring run up and down a few hills was exactly what was called for. I took the four-wheel-drive track over the hill to Loch Cuin, aiming to run back along the loch side to the edge of the village, which would then allow me either to turn for home or to add on the hill road if I hadn't run enough.

I'd only covered about two miles when I heard a voice. Over the pounding of my heart it was indistinct, but I stopped and turned. Coming up the track from the south was Ewan, towing a reluctant Molly, who was far more interested in the intriguing smells in the ditch than in anything resembling exercise. I waited, leaning on my knees and panting. Now I'd stopped, I felt the heat rise into my face: I knew it would be hard to get started again.

When Ewan caught up I didn't bother to talk, but simply fell into place beside him, and we walked up the hill together. Ewan eyed my glowing countenance and said nothing, but Molly had no such compunctions. She pushed up against me and licked my sweaty hands, butting her head against my legs to get closer to those lovely (to dogs at least) sweaty smells. Ewan bent and took her off the leash. There was no risk of her running off and worrying livestock – she simply couldn't be bothered.

The dog ambled off to sniff an interesting cowpat. We wandered on in quiet companionship until we reached the ridge-crest, and gazed north-west along the length of the loch toward the sea. A long bank of cloud draped itself over the hills above Quinish, on the other side of the loch, mimicking the shape of the landscape beneath. The wind dropped and I could hear the low hum of bees, making their way from clover to clover around our feet.

I sat down and wrapped my arms around my knees. After

stretching his long arms toward the sky, Ewan joined me. I looked at him. "I've been thinking about something you said when we were out fishing," I said. Ewan turned his head to me. "Your grandfather pulled something up out of his nets: a bit of twisted metal that turned out to be weighing scales?"

He nodded, and I went on: "It was exactly the sort of thing that Norse traders might have been carrying about: taking their payment in weight of metal, rather than in any particular coin."

"Aye," said Ewan. It was pleasant thinking aloud to someone so peaceful. It was not that he wasn't interested: his eyes never left mine. It was just that he was content to listen, until he had something to say.

"Where did he find it? Was it near where he lived, at Haunn?"

"Ah," said Ewan. "No, it wasn't. He was right round north of the island: in a sheltered bit where he'd often found good fishing when the wind was in a particular corner. It's not easy to find from the land side, since the forestry planted up that whole block. But from the sea it's just around to the north-east of Calgary. There used to be a village there in the old days, but the signs of it are long gone. Even in my grandfather's day it had been empty for a generation."

I was excited. "The scales might be contemporary with my chess queen. They could have come from the same place. A current along the top of the island might sweep things out of that cove, and land them on Calgary. Perhaps there was a shipwreck there, and your grandfather pulled the scales up out of the wreckage. Perhaps that is where my little queen came from."

"Could be," said Ewan, slowly. "It could very well be." He hauled himself to his feet, and whistled for Molly. "It looks like rain," he said.

I glanced up the loch toward the sea. Visibility had decreased markedly, and a sheet of rain was sweeping down the loch towards us. "Okay," I said, jumping up.

Molly came to heel, and loped beside Ewan as we ran down the hill. Ewan's route ran past my house, and he slowed to keep pace with me until we reached the gate: just as the sky fell. "Come in," I gasped. "No use running on in this: wait till it passes over." Ewan nodded, and together we followed the path by the wall, and turned into the porch. Molly shook herself all over us as we pulled off our top layers (my fleece in need of wringing after even such a short exposure), and I opened the door into the cool and newly cleaned interior. Molly made herself at home in front of the fire, even though it was not lit, nor likely to be, and immediately went to sleep. She had developed the same knack as her elderly master of sleeping at a moment's notice, whenever the opportunity presented itself.

Ewan and I stopped in the kitchen, while I put the kettle on. He reached over to the coat-rack, and pulled down another fleece to put round my shoulders. I discovered that I was shivering and pulled the warm clothing round myself gratefully. As I reached for the tea-caddy, I realised Ewan was still standing very close behind me.

I half-turned, wondering what might be wrong, when I was surprised by his gentle grasp on my shoulders. As I put my head back to look up at him, his mouth came down to meet mine. I felt a jolt of pleasure pass right through me, rooting me to the ground, and I leaned into him, feeling the length of his body against mine, and the hard line of the kitchen workbench against my back. His thumbs worked up and down the back of my neck, stroking my hairline, and I closed my eyes and pushed my hands up against his chest. He drew back slightly and looked at me.

"If you want me to go, now is the time to say so," he said quietly.

"In this rain?" I laughed, and he grinned.

It seemed strange to turn back and make the tea, as if nothing had happened. Ewan leaned on the bench and made no move to touch me, but I felt his glance as a feather-touch on my skin. As I automatically squeezed tea bags and poured milk, I could still feel the hardness of his nipples in the centre of my palms. When he shifted his weight, the movement of air between us was a physical force, and when he brushed my arm in taking the cup, I trembled. He met my eye; a long, slow look, then he set down his tea and took me in his arms again.

This time he was thorough, and by the end of the kiss I was aroused in a way that I had never been before. I felt shy and inexperienced, and very nervous about admitting it, but the quiet communication between us didn't seem to need explanations, and I basked in the sensations of my body, and its powerful messages of need and desire. I looked down at Ewan's feet as I unbuttoned his shirt, and slid my hands inside, feeling the smoothness of his skin.

I tried to ignore feelings of vulnerability as he eased my blouse off my shoulders and deftly undid my bra. He laid his cheek alongside mine and held the small of my back against one strong warm hand, while the other explored each breast in turn. "Lovely," he said, and bent his mouth to them. I made a decision and took his hand, and he followed without a word as I led him up to the bedroom.

When I lay down on the bed, the sheets were cool against my superheated skin. It felt strange to be touching another human being, and when I opened my mouth to say so my voice sounded shockingly loud in my ears. Its sound brought me back to earth a little, and I became aware of Ewan's long, rangy body alongside me, and felt the heat of him against my skin. I lifted myself up on one arm and looked at him.

Ewan stopped stroking me, and lay back on the pillow. He looked back at me, silent and still, and waited patiently. I became aware that I felt no guilt, no fear, no need to be reluctant. What was happening here was something so right that I wondered that I had never experienced it before. My inner voice muttered its doubt, but I overrode it.

I leaned over Ewan and rubbed my face on his chest and

stomach, then ran my fingers over his body, taking in the shape and the heat of him. He sighed happily, and gave himself over to it, but after a few minutes took up his active role again. I wanted to fight it: I felt mildly guilty that I should be the one receiving all the pleasure, but Ewan's movements and involuntary sounds told me he was enjoying what he was doing as much as I was enjoying receiving it.

I let my head fall back onto the pillow, and stroked his arms and head lightly as I sank into the languorous, liquid warmth of his tongue on my skin. Time became an endless well of delight into which I fell, diving through fathoms of warm, silk water into the deep red darkness of pleasure. Eventually I fell so deep that sleep took me, in the breath between pleasure and the next soothing moment of satiated desire.

When I woke, the room was cool with the coming of dusk. There was no body in the bed beside me and, when I grabbed my dressing-gown and went downstairs, the man and the dog were gone. I hugged the dressing-gown round myself, and went to make some dinner. The automatic process of choosing and preparing a meal settled me back into normality: I felt the strange dislocation of sexual pleasure receding into my subconscious, and began to feel instead its comfortable aftermath.

This must be how it's meant to be. My body had performed as it should, and its animal awareness reminded me that the life of the mind isn't everything: even the movement of my mouth as I chewed and swallowed, and the message of relieved hunger from my stomach, were small flickers of satisfaction enhancing the remembered experience of a great delight. I felt very pleased with myself. As I ate I reflected that I had undoubtedly received far more pleasure than I had given, and wondered if Ewan would give me the opportunity to reciprocate. I hoped so.

Later, as I climbed the stairs to bed, the front door opened, and I stood trying not to breath, so as to identify the quiet sounds I heard. Almost at once, a tall figure appeared at the bottom of the stairs, and softly called my name. "Come up," I said, and turned away into the bedroom. A small, crabbed, unconfident voice told me I was taking him for granted. (You don't know he's come to make love again. Do you really think you were that good?)

He was already taking off his jacket as he came through the door, and in short order he had me in his arms, and I was pulling him down on top of me. A resourceful man, Ewan had been home for a packet of condoms, and quickly showed that he still wanted me. I wrapped my legs around him and let myself go: this was no reluctant lover. Ewan came quickly the first time, rolling me over on top of him afterwards, and cradling me on his chest until his breathing slowed.

The second time I rode him, swaying, rocking, rising and falling while he tickled my nipples, caressed my stomach and stroked me until I reached my own climax. As I fell forward over him he began to shudder again, but we were both dripping with sweat before he had finished.

Ewan's voice rumbled into my ear, not language so much as a wordless sound of appreciation. It vibrated through my head, pressed against his chest while I listened to the drumming of his heartbeat. I let my weight slip off him and curled up in his arm, smelling the male scent of him as I began to doze. I felt comfortable in every pore, and the muscle of his thigh, as I stroked it, was soft with relaxation. I closed my eyes and drifted away into sleep again.

This time I woke to the grey light of dawn, and an insistent rain drumming on the roof. Ewan was gone again, but the aching languor of seldom-used muscles told their own story. I stretched luxuriously and rose in body: most of my mind seemed to be still wrapped in a kind of rosy fog, which persisted through breakfast (very late) and a feeble attempt to deal with some bills and accounts. My mind wasn't on the job. In the middle of another long, slow reverie I suddenly remembered: Sam!

I ran for the car, getting soaked twice as I opened and then closed the gate behind it. For the umpteenth time I swore I was going to invest in a cattle grid, but put it out of mind as I threw the car into gear and raced for Craignure. With the best will in the world, I arrived twenty minutes after the ferry had docked. Sam stood by the road with his backpack beside him. The Calmac office was open, so his choice to wait in the rain did not bode well. He threw his pack in the back and climbed in, staring straight ahead out of the windscreen without a word. Drips from his sodden hair ran down his face, and he wiped his eyes with the back of his hand.

I groped behind the driver's seat with one hand, dragged out a slightly grubby but dry towel and handed it to my son. He grunted, his body language eased a little, and we travelled the rest of the way without conversation. I apologised again for being late, but made no explanation, and nothing more was said until we arrived home.

At first, I had expected Sam to be angry, and viewed his silence as punishment for my neglect, but as he pushed into the house ahead of me and I heard his sigh, and saw his shoulders slump, I began to recognise that something more serious was going on. I quietly made up two mugs of sweet hot chocolate and brought them into the living room, handed one to Sam and went off to find a blanket.

By the time I got back he had set the drink aside and towelled his hair dry, and as I laid the blanket on his shoulder he pulled it gratefully around himself. He did not pick up his mug again. I sat down at the other end of the sofa with my feet curled under me, sipped my own drink, and waited.

16

After a few minutes Sam groaned and put his head in his hands. I set down my cup and regarded him calmly, but he didn't speak, so I decided to. "How was your trip with Dad?"

Sam jolted upright. "Dad?" he shouted, "That idiot. He's such a poser." His face flushed and the story tumbled out of him. His overreaction was so unexpected that I lost the thread of what he was saying.

"...and he was late picking me up in Oban. Said he'd run into weather problems, which didn't make any sense, because the Sound of Mull was like a millpond. It was probably another one of Dad's excuses for not being on time.

"I thought we'd be sailing. You know - I'd packed all my old clothes, and the good waterproofs. I was all set for a week of raising sails and coiling sheets. I suppose I realised there'd be a skipper – Dad's not that experienced at sailing – and maybe some crew, but I still thought it was all about us going sailing together."

I picked up my cup again. It gave my fingers something to do. "So, if it wasn't a sailing trip, what was it?"

"Well, the 'yacht' turned out to be this dirty great motorboat. I mean, really big. We had a cabin each and there were berths for the skipper and crew as well. I could see straight away that the trip was going to be more like cruising than sailing. The crew didn't need any help from me, that's for sure, and then there were the girls."

I sat up and paid attention.

"There were two of them. At first I thought they were sisters – they kind of looked like each other – but then I found out that one of them was from Germany and the other one was from Bulgaria. They were nice enough, and at first I thought they were part of the crew. They didn't come up on deck much; they weren't exactly dressed for west of Scotland weather. Mostly they stayed in the main cabin and made drinks, and played card games with each other.

"The one from Bulgaria's called Anna. I'm pretty sure she's Dad's new girlfriend. Every time he came in she would drape herself over him and call him pet names. She knew just how he liked his drinks fixed. The other one, Katja, was German, but I found out her Mum came from Slovenia. She was nice. She taught me some neat card tricks too."

"Wait a minute. Are you telling me you were on some kind of playboy yacht?"

"That's exactly what I'm saying. I thought we were going to sail round the islands together, just the two of us plus maybe the crew. Instead, it was this great, shiny, pretentious *thing* with flags all over it.

"Dad kept disappearing into his cabin with Anna, and leaving me and Katja alone. To start with I went up on deck and hung out there, but it was pretty boring. It's not like there was anything for me to do. I asked Dad if he had any binoculars, in case I saw whales, but he told me to stop wasting my time. That wasn't why he'd brought me along.

"Then I remembered that he'd said he would introduce me to some interesting people, and I asked him when we were going to meet them. He just laughed in a weird way, and told me I already had. In the end, it was Katja who told me what was going on. He'd hired her to persuade me to lose my virginity with her."

"What?"

"Yeah, that's pretty much what I said. I asked him about it and he admitted it straight away. He said he'd interviewed a hundred girls to pick out the one who was perfect for me. He said it was time I was made a man, and it was up to him to provide this rite of passage. He talked about Katja like she was some kind of…what's the word for something you buy?"

"Commodity."

"Yeah, just like something you pick up from the shops. That's not right, is it, Mum? I mean, Katja was really nice, and pretty, and smart too. We definitely started to become friends. But I kept telling Dad that I would want the first time to be special. I'd want it to be with someone I knew.

"He said I'd been hanging round too long with that…with you. He said it was time I manned up."

"For God's sake, he's gone too far this time." I couldn't believe what I was hearing. Even for Drew this was incomprehensible behaviour.

"Calm down, Mum. Nothing actually happened. I told Katja that I'd already lost my virginity. I made her promise not to tell Dad, but she came up with an idea. She decided to go to Dad and tell him that I wasn't a virgin, but that I didn't want to sleep with her because I didn't fancy her. She said that he'd be more likely to leave me alone if he thought I'd already done it with someone.

"Dad asked me about it – he wanted to know if I preferred blondes, and I said I did. Then he told me I shouldn't trust 'that little piece Katherine' (he meant Katja) because she'd spoken to him behind my back. He said 'You can't rely on these girls. You think they're honest, but it only lasts as long as you're paying them.' It was such a mean thing to say."

I took a deep breath. I wanted nothing more than to go out and kill Drew with my bare hands, for dragging my son into such a sordid situation. "It was clever of you to get Katja to tell Dad you weren't a virgin. He might not have believed you if you'd said it yourself."

"Katja said the best way to deal with someone like Dad is to tell him the truth, always. That way if you ever need to lie, for some really important reason like saving your life, they're more likely to believe you."

"Sam, what are you saying?"

His face was colourless and his eyes as grey as the wool of his blanket. He evaded my question. "Can I have my cocoa warmed up?"

My hands were shaking as I heated the milk. I couldn't tell if it was shock or rage. I wanted to focus on my anger with Drew, but a nasty, cold suspicion kept getting in the way. What if Sam had been telling the truth to Drew?

Sam went upstairs and changed into dry clothes, but when he came back down he settled into the same, defensive position on the sofa. He clutched the mug I gave him, and I held my own like a talisman while I waited. At first, I thought he wasn't going to tell me anything more, but after a few minutes I saw him visibly take his courage in his hands. He raised his head and met my eye.

"Mum, I'm going to tell you something. I really need you to hear this. Please promise you'll let me speak, and not interrupt me. I just need you to listen."

I stared at him, wanting to demand more, to hold off making promises until I knew what I was getting into, but some instinct said no. "I'm listening. I promise not to interrupt."

He began to speak, and the story he told was simple, understandable: even predictable, if you'd ever allowed yourself to consider the possibility in the first place. I reeled under it.

"Do you remember the International Club?" I did. Sam had been studying for his first round of external exams. I knew that even without the crisis of separation and divorce going on all around him, he would have difficult in gaining really good marks. Being at boarding school protected him from the worst of it, but I was aware that he was struggling. So I was delighted when he emailed to say that he had signed up for two after-school tutorial clubs.

These clubs were run by senior students, for the benefit of juniors, and although nominally under the supervision of teachers, they were thought to be more successful if the hand on the helm was light, and the boys left to sort out their own approaches to the work.

The Geography and English club (otherwise known as the International Club, since all three of its tutors were overseas students) had gone very well. Sam had begun to receive glowing reports from his teachers, and there's no doubt his exam results benefited from the extra tuition.

"I don't think I told you, but there was a Maths club as well. Only two of us signed up for it, and there were two seniors running the club, so they just picked one each. It made sense. Each of us could get individual tuition, and we didn't need to use a classroom, because we could just do it in the senior students' rooms.

"I was working with Magnus Welch. He was seventeen. He was absolutely brilliant at Maths. He taught me heaps of stuff I didn't know, and helped me get better at the things I could already do."

I did remember. Not about the club, but Sam had emailed me about his improvements in Maths and he'd mentioned the older boy who was helping him. My assumption had been that Sam had developed a crush on the boy; he definitely seemed to look up to him. I wondered what this Maths club had to do with Sam's experience on the yacht with Drew. Sam seemed to be talking about something completely different.

Eventually, the emails from school had petered out, and I'd gone back to making do with our regular Friday night phone calls. Sam had seemed quiet, and nothing more was said about the tutorial clubs. Exams were looming and I had focused on talking about nothing, as mothers sometimes need to do when all the available 'somethings' are fraught with tension.

I left him alone to deal with his worries, content that the school system was good, and that I would pick up the pieces when he came home for the holidays. It hadn't worked out that way. That had been the holiday from hell, when Sam hardly spoke a word except to fight, and Drew's demands to have the boy intruded into almost every day.

That terrible winter break led directly to my plans for sand-sculptures and decorating this summer. Ironically, my organised programme of activities had been completely hijacked by the spontaneous events following discovery of the chess piece. Despite its anti-climatic end, the archaeological mystery had captured his imagination in a way that no planned activity could ever have done.

Sam was still talking, and now I began to allow myself to understand what he was saying.

"Magnus was tutoring me twice a week in his room. It was much quieter and more private than the common room. We did all the ordinary stuff, and then Magnus started teaching me the Maths he was working on. Calculus and Integration is brilliant. It all made sense when Magnus explained it. He's a really good teacher. We became good friends, too. You wouldn't believe how much we have in common."

He stopped, and met my eyes. I smiled, to show I was still listening.

"One day we were studying fractal diagrams. You know – Mandelbrot sets and all that stuff?"

I shook my head. Maths had never been my strong suit.

"Magnus was sitting behind me. I could feel his breath on the back of my neck. Then he stroked it, with the back of his hand. I looked at him. I wasn't sure, you see. He was, though. He kissed me."

I felt all the little hairs on the back of my neck stand up. I shivered with a sense of horrified revulsion that I didn't want to analyse, as I relived the sensation of Ewan's thumbs stroking up and down my hairline as we kissed. This was the last thing I would have imagined, when Sam had started talking. I felt tears welling up behind my eyes as I studied the face of my son, willing my face to keep still, while behind it a little voice in my head began to wail. "Stop! I don't want to hear this. I don't want to deal with any of it. Take it away."

I struggled to think of something sensible to say. "Um. What...?"

By then Sam's own self-control had cracked, and the tears were streaming down his face. "Mum, we had sex," he said. "I had sex with another boy, and I liked it. Dad kept saying he didn't want me to become a little limp-wrist, but I already am." Hot tears of rage and frustration poured down his face, and in the middle of them, his terrified eyes stared at me, waiting for rejection.

I stared back, memorising every pore of the beloved face. No matter what I said or did, our relationship was changed forever. My child had grown up, right before my eyes, and I was deluged with a torrent of emotions I wasn't ready to assimilate. I tried to marshal my thoughts. A jumble of questions rattled in my head, and I pushed most of them to one side. This wasn't the time for me to reveal my fears, or for that matter the anger that shook me. Whatever I said, I needed to be very careful not to damage the raw and bleeding wound my son had exposed to me.

I reached forward and took Sam's hand in mine. He flinched, then glanced down at the hanky I pressed into it. He blew his nose loudly and scrubbed his eyes with his sleeve.

"My love," I said, "don't give yourself names that belong in the mouths of intolerance and fear. If you are gay, then be proud of it. You are who you are; and as long as you treat your partners with love and respect, then you are as good a person as you can be."

I bit back all the questions I wanted to ask. "Did you use protection?"; "What kind of person is Magnus? Has he done this sort of thing before?"; "What is wrong with that school? They were supposed to protect you." The worst one of all, though, was the question that had forced its way into my head as soon as Sam had begun to deliver his revelation: "What about me? What about my grandchildren?"

With this realisation, my anger turned inward and I

understood myself. I had expected to mould Sam to meet my expectations for the future. Here was the root of my anger: the frustrated belief that my barrenness would be relieved in the next generation, by the production of grandchildren. How arrogant.

I let myself consider confronting the other unspoken issue: Sam had been only fifteen. Technically, the other boy's action was rape. I could report this as a crime. I could insist on prosecution. I could drag my vulnerable teenager into the police station and the witness box, and make him bare his soul before strangers. I could confront the school, and demand they investigate. Doing so would cause Sam misery, and harm the trust between us, and there was no guarantee Magnus would be convicted of anything other than poor self-control and normal, adolescent risk-taking behaviour.

Reluctantly, I let that go. A good memory, albeit experienced at an earlier age than I would have liked, is better than a memory sullied by adult overreaction afterwards. Hadn't I learned that lesson myself? There was no way to undo what had happened six months ago. All we could do now was to go forward, and accept what had already happened.

"Sam, I hope you've been lucky, and there won't be any further consequences. I'll admit your story has frightened me: it's a dangerous road you'll be treading, especially in this part of the world. Scotland isn't the most tolerant nation. But I'm glad you've found this out about yourself, and I'll support you, whatever you decide to do in the future. I love you. I'll always be here if you need me."

By the end of this speech I was crying as well, and Sam shuffled forward and threw his arms around me. He clung to me like the child he still was, but within a few moments he pulled away again. He sat up straight, wiped his face and straightened his shoulders, already putting himself into the role of the man he was to become. He handed me the damp hanky and I blew my nose, loudly. I caught his eye, and we both laughed in relief.

"I spent all the Christmas break worrying about what would happen when I went back to school. Would he still want me? What would I do if I didn't want him? What if someone found out?

"When I got back to school, Magnus wasn't there. I asked David (the other Maths club senior) about it. He told me Magnus had moved to another school. I don't know which one.

"I kept watching the domestics, and the other boys' mums, and Matron! I couldn't imagine ever wanting to have sex with a girl, but I didn't fancy any of the other boys, either. I wondered if Magnus had done something to me, to stop me wanting anyone else. That's not it, though."

I stirred, but he went on without giving me the chance to speak. "I thought a lot about what you and Dad would want. Like having children and stuff. I knew that didn't feel right, and when I went on the boat with Dad I was finally sure. I am gay. I don't think I want to have any more relationships, though. At least, not until I finish school. It's too complicated. What will Dad do?"

I gazed with love at my own greatest complication. One moment prognosticating on his future with certainty, and the next assuming I can read someone else's mind for him. Not to mention dealing in one breath with the whole range of fears, desires and expectations that I had held for him: 'children and stuff'.

"I don't know what Dad will say or do," I said sombrely. "I think you already know he'll find it difficult, but we will weather it. No-one can take away your belief in yourself. You must have done a lot of thinking about this, without anyone to advise you. It's no wonder you were such a grumpy so-and-so last winter. I never imagined it was anything to do with school, let alone with a relationship. I thought it was me and Dad making you miserable. There you were growing up under my nose, and I didn't notice a thing. I think you can carry this off, through the rest of school and into your adult life. Just stop and think for a moment if you're ever uncertain, and your heart will tell you what to do. That's good advice for everything, not just sex."

"Mum," said Sam fondly. "You're such a romantic."

"I shall consider that a compliment," I said. For a moment we sat and looked at each other. I felt my mouth quirk. "Playboy yacht," I said. Suddenly we were both consumed with laughter, tears streaming down our faces.

"Oh my God, Mum," said Sam. "What is he like?"

Now the storm was over, I hoisted myself to my feet. Sam blew his nose and folded the blanket neatly before laying it over the back of the sofa.

"Thanks, Mum," he said soberly, following me out to the kitchen.

"You're welcome," I said. "But next time don't make me sweat through a holiday like last Christmas. If you've got something on your mind I'd rather you blurted it out straight away. Anyway, I'm off to make dinner now. I won't ask what you want – you can eat what you're given!"

17

Overnight, life took on a new calmness. With only a couple of weeks left before Sam went back to start his last year at school, he was hard at work on his Geography project. He hogged the computer for hours at a time, sending and receiving e-mails, and typing enthusiastically with two fingers. I wandered about the house tidying, or weeded the garden fitfully, and tried to encompass the new relationship I was forging with my only son.

The feelings of frustration and helplessness I'd felt on learning of Sam's seduction by his schoolmate hadn't faded much, but I still felt warmed by his willingness to trust in me. I was proud of the way he'd dealt with his experience on the boat with his Dad. If I was going to take out my frustrations on anyone, then Drew was a prime target. What an idiotic trick to pull. I didn't feel any need to criticise Sam, although I still worried about him.

There was a new closeness in our day-to-day dealings. He seemed to have overcome his temper outbursts – or no longer felt the need for them, now his great secret was out. But I felt a gap had opened between us that would probably never be bridged again. Sam had shown himself capable of handling a major problem alone for months. If it wasn't for Drew's stupid intervention he might not have told me at all, and he was already stepping confidently into adult independence. And I, who had mentally prepared myself for years to cope when Sam became an adult, found I wasn't ready at all.

Most of all I feared Sam no longer needed me, and that was a hard feeling to face. This was like the pain of his first term at school, or perhaps more like watching his tiny form through the wall of his incubator, forbidden to hold him. That thought was a revelation: I was grieving for the loss of my baby. When I found myself dusting the pictures for the third time I downed tools and took myself off to visit Bernie. A good dose of nappies, other people's housework and the smell of baby sick is the best cure for rose-tinted memories of one's own child.

Emma Jane (nee Tiny) was cute but loud, and Tilly and Tom had been packed off to their grandmother again, to get (and give) a little peace and quiet. Bernie lay back on pillows in the living room, looking pale and thin-cheeked, and wisely said nothing while I fussed around her. At last, she stirred and called over to the kitchen, where I was scrubbing the grill pan.

"Ready to talk yet?" she said. "I'd like tea, at least, and you need to stop. In fact, I'm ordering you to stop. Come and sit, and if you don't want to tell me anything then you can put up with my tales of woe."

I smiled at her, and obediently made the tea. I already had a batch of cakes in the oven, and they were ready at exactly the right moment. Bernie popped a steaming cake into her mouth and gasped. "Itsh the currantsh," she said indistinctly. "They're hot!"

I sat and sipped my tea, settling back into the cushions with a sigh. It felt good to sit down with a friend – someone who would not be judgmental, or at least whose judgment would be fair and helpful. Bernie regarded me expectantly.

"I hardly know where to start," I said. "Perhaps you'd better tell me your gory details first."

"Gory, hell," said Bernie. "It was all over in five minutes. You know the wretched child hung on to the last minute and beyond. When she did arrive, it was instant panic. One moment I was hanging out washing, and the next I was grabbing my bits and holding her in. Jed hardly had time to call the midwife, let alone tell her what was going on, before Emma had slithered out and taken centre stage. Fiona turned up in time to cut the cord and fill out the forms, but that was about it. I just lay back and let it all happen."

I winced. "Surely that must have hurt?" I asked.

"That's the understatement of the century. It was all the work of second stage compressed into a few minutes. I've never felt anything like it, and I never want to again. It was like having a piano dropped on you, or going over Niagara Falls without the barrel. Scary, but at the same time it was incredibly exciting. I just stepped outside my poor torn body and watched myself ride the rapids: white-water rafting on a river as big as the universe. It was only when it was all over that I got the shakes, and had to be babied myself.

"I'd had a tummy ache all day, and that must have been first stage. With the other two, the early stages of labour were ghastly and went on for hours, but this time it happened without me noticing. All of a sudden, she was ready to arrive, and I had *no* say in it. Incredible."

Emma Jane squawked, and I bent down and lifted her from her basket. I nuzzled the baby's downy cheek before handing her over to her mother. Bernie tucked the child under her sweater and she began feeding without fuss. For a moment, I felt jealous of Bernie: because of the baby? Or because Bernie had such an amazing experience giving birth to her? And then again, all the signs were that they were being well cared for by her loving family: the house hadn't really been dirty, the other children were in good company, and Bernie herself, despite being pale and tired, was looking wonderful.

I felt a wave of bitter loneliness sweep over me: why had I made such bad choices? Then I remembered Bernie's own stories about the beginning of her marriage to Jed: it hadn't been such a bed of roses then. And although it might be fair to take some of the blame for how my relationship with Drew had turned out, I couldn't blame myself for what had happened at Sam's birth, or for my inability to have any more children. I sighed, and Bernie was immediately aware.

"Speak up, honey," she said brusquely. "No use feeling sorry for yourself: tell Auntie Bernie."

I put my head in my hands and breathed in the warm redness behind my closed lids. "I don't know where to start," I mumbled indistinctly.

"Start somewhere round the edges, and we'll work our way into the middle," suggested Bernie. I glanced at her, expecting a facetious grin, and got it. "It doesn't matter where you start," my friend said. "Tell me anything." The grin had given way to a quiet, sympathetic expression that I leaned into as if it was a warm wind, or the sun on my face.

"Sam is gay," I said, and stopped.

Bernie waited, saying nothing. Her expression had not changed. I felt a little let down: I had expected at least a gasp of surprise. Bernie's phlegmatic expression stirred me into speech.

"All those years you spend bringing up a child. You think you know them. I haven't even had other children to distract me. I thought I knew everything about Sam, but I had no idea. You should have been there, Bernie. The look on my face must have been priceless. I sat there, telling myself not to react, trying to keep my face still. How could that have happened without my knowing? Mothers are supposed to know these things."

Bernie sat quietly for a moment before she spoke. "How did you deal with it?" she asked.

"Oh, I told him it was okay, I wasn't going to reject him, we'd work it out somehow, and he was going to be all right: all that sort of thing. But I feel so sick, Bernie. How could this have happened?"

"How could what have happened?"

"Sam's made a choice that will affect the whole of his life. Wherever he goes he'll always have to fear intolerance and bigotry, he's more likely to encounter violence or abuse, he'll find it hard to find a partner, he's at higher risk of disease, he might have trouble getting a job or finding a place to live. And if he brings a friend home I'll never know whether I should be greeting them as just a mate, or as his Mate. If you know what I mean."

I glanced at Bernie, expecting to see her sympathetic listening expression. Instead, Bernie's face was creased with anger. I was shocked.

"Listen to yourself," said Bernie, sharply. "It sounds to me as though you've written Sam off already, if you're mapping out such a bleak future for him. Stop and think again: Sam's a wonderful, warm, intelligent person with the ability to work for whatever he wants in this life, and a great capacity for making friends. His sexuality, however you define it, is only a small part of his life, and you can't pigeon-hole his whole future because one part of his make-up doesn't fit your expectations. As for saying he has *chosen* this…!"

"What do you mean?"

"Answer me this: did you make Sam homosexual?"

I gasped. "I…no." I said. "That is—"

"Then accept that nothing you can do will make him heterosexual. It is not in your power to influence this, and it's not in Sam's power either. He is a whole and independent personality, and his sexuality is a part of that, as I am quite sure you will recognise when you stop feeling sorry for yourself. I can't accept that you genuinely believe Sam's future is blighted by this discovery. There must be something in your own experience that leads you to fear this."

Bernie glared at me challengingly, but relented when she saw the tears in my eyes. I was numbed by her words, and found myself thrust back into the memory of Sam's revelation, and my feelings at the time. I saw again the terrified expression on his face as he revealed his greatest vulnerability, and felt a rush of tenderness at the trust he'd put in me. He'd shown strength and maturity. Surely I could trust him to make sensible decisions about his own future or, if he made foolish decisions, to be capable of dealing with them and making the best of things. Actually, on balance he was probably acting more sensibly than I had at the same age.

"You're right," I said. "I was blaming myself that Sam has turned out this way, and that's because I believed it was a bad thing, something that would harm him. I'm his Mum, and I'm supposed to protect him from harm. But I can't protect him from this."

"No," murmured Bernie, "and nor should you. This is part of Sam's adult life, and all you can do is to decide whether you will reject him or support him. You know you've already made that choice."

I nodded, then hid my head in my hands again as my face crumpled. A sound burst from my throat and tears poured through my fingers, releasing a lifetime of care and worry for my son. At first, I couldn't stop, and the feeling was cathartic. In the process I let go the need to control him, recognising it as the manifestation of my fear of being alone. Sam was going from me, like it or not, and if I tried to hold onto him I would only lose him sooner.

As soon as I recognised and faced this, I saw my own bleak, sad future stretching ahead of me, no longer mitigated by the cosy expectation of living vicariously through my child and the future I had planned for him. I couldn't continue to depend on Sam for the emotional support he had given me, or to use him as the repository of all my pent-up affection and love.

I gulped, and scrubbed my eyes with my fists. I felt light-headed, but also light of spirit: freed from the tremendous burden of guilt I had felt over Sam's future, and a little way further along the journey of discovering myself. I hugged Bernie gently.

"Thank you. You always see through my stupid ideas, and put me back on the right track."

"Stupid ideas are my speciality," said Bernie, squeezing me back. "Next time it'll be my turn to trot out my half-baked prejudices, and you can shoot me down." I looked at her, to see how serious she was being and she grinned at me, and then sobered. "I didn't mean to hurt you," she said. "I knew you didn't really mean it."

"I know. It didn't hurt any more than it needed to. You were completely right, as always. Thanks." I hugged her again, and let her go.

"You're welcome, my love," said my good friend, surreptitiously drying a few tears of her own. "Come by any time: you know we love to see you here."

I left Bernie in the warmth of her kitchen, chopping vegetables with the baby in a carrypack on her front, and headed home in the half-light of summer dusk, dodging the midges as I reached my own front door. Sam came out as I was going in, nearly knocking me over as he barged through the door.

"Sorry, Mum," he said. "Ewan's picking me up at the road end. I'm going out to crew for him tomorrow – he's taking a boatload to Tiree for the weekend, and I'm going to be galley slave. He's paying me minimum wage, but it'll be great experience. I'll be back on Monday morning. See you."

By the end of this speech, he had reached the gate and closed it behind him. I was left standing open-mouthed in the doorway, absently scratching at a growing crop of midge bites. I came to myself and called: "Did Ewan have any message for me?"

"No. Were you expecting one?" Sam's voice was casual and unsuspecting.

"No, not really. Have a good time. Call me if you need me." I couldn't think of anything meaningful to say. My newly independent adult had fledged and gone – and I had almost missed his first flight. He disappeared into the growing dusk and I heard the beep of a horn, followed by a door slamming and the sound of a car driving away. Gone.

18

I closed the door and sat down on the kitchen floor. For a long time I stared at the wall, with its silly frieze of daft-looking sea creatures. What to do? What to think? Was Sam running away from reality, or making a sensible decision about work and money? It would do him good to have earned some money of his own this summer, but what about his schoolwork? Had I ever been this precipitous? Answer: yes. I married Drew after about two minute's consideration. In the end, the decision to leave him was just as sudden. Between one breath and the next, the intention had crystallized, and from that moment until my arrival on Mull I had been running at light speed. If Sam is impetuous, at least I can admit he comes by it honestly.

Oh, well. I relaxed a little. If I let go my attachment to Sam's schoolwork and trust he will either have done it, or be prepared to face the consequences, then there's nothing left to worry about. He's gone to crew on a well-managed boat skippered by someone I know and trust, and no doubt the experience will do him nothing but good. Also, it gives me the whole weekend to think about myself…and Ewan.

Yes. There was a thought big enough to keep me going all weekend. Making love with Ewan had been driven from my mind in the aftermath of Sam's revelation, but I had nonetheless been a little surprised that he hadn't contacted me. It was what I think I would have done, if our positions had been reversed, and it hadn't occurred to me that Ewan would have seen our lovemaking as anything other than the joyous beginning of a new relationship.

I had expected we would see each other again, quite soon, and that our friends and relations would gradually become aware we were together. He was no longer Ewan MacInnes the skipper of *Martha-Margaret*, who sometimes takes us fishing, but Ewan MacInnes My Lover. However, his failure to call me, or even leave a message through Sam, had definitely dented his saintly image.

Perhaps he was waiting for me to call him? How was this going to work? It's not as though we'd been in the habit of calling each other before this happened.

I fantasised about picking up the phone to find Ewan at the other end. What would he say? I couldn't imagine him saying anything. Starting a conversation about a relationship that might or might not be happening would be far outside his comfort zone. It was much more likely he would turn up on my doorstep one day, and things would happen. Or not happen. Just as I might be out for a run, one day, and he might join me. We've never arranged things in advance, or even discussed how or why we started running together. It's just one of those things that started happening, felt okay, and continued in an ad hoc, unplanned, totally unpredictable way.

Could I cope with a sexual relationship run on that basis? Thinking about it made me feel vulnerable and hypersensitive. On what basis was I assuming there was going to be a relationship? I had been very young when I tied myself to Drew, and I really have no idea how these things evolve, even when the parties are comfortable talking to one another.

I wandered through the house aimlessly, picking things up and putting them down. I held the little plastic warder and peered at him, missing the weight and heft of the real chess piece. This little guy had nothing useful to tell me, and I set him down again.

At last, I ended up in the bathroom, and eyed myself in the mirror. I angled the mirror downward so that I couldn't see my face and started to remove my clothes. I kept my eyes lowered until I was completely naked, then raised them and examined myself. Pale. Well, I was always going to be pale unless sunburned. I never really take a tan, even in the sunniest of summers. Short. The nice word is petite, although I'm not really petite. Almost average height for a woman, but my legs are relatively short compared to my body. Shorter than anything you see in a magazine or on TV. (Cassandra Longmore, don't even start on self-image and the media. We could be here all night.) Best I can say is that I'm okay.

A nice face: snub nose could be said to give it charm. A good, healthy body. No one would guess I'd had a child – only the faint white Caesarean scar marked my abdomen; Sam had been so small when he was born that I had no stretch marks at all. Small breasts (small but perfectly formed) and a small, round tummy. I like my breasts. They're big enough to be there, but not so big as to cause me problems. I well remember Bernie's frequent moans about the misery of large breasts – backache, neck ache, blouses that gaped and men who couldn't look her in the eye because they felt compelled to talk to the chest. I'd never had any trouble talking with men. Never felt threatened or disconcerted by any inappropriate interest. I suppose I always felt myself to be off limits, Drew's property, and therefore unavailable for dalliance. Except for that lovely librarian. Mmm.

Perhaps it was a matter of pheromones. I don't feel any different, but I seem to be attracting a different response from men. Niall? Maybe, or perhaps he became friendlier as a result of getting to know me better. Those men at the Post Office definitely looked. They've looked before – it's not a look I ever got while I was married to Drew. At least, if men looked, I didn't notice. Ewan hadn't seduced me with words. All it took was a look, a touch. His seduction of me was a conversation without words. Or does he feel I seduced him?

At the time, it seemed the only way to act, as if our bodies had made their own agreement and no discussion was necessary. I recalled the feeling of his hand cradling my head, and the weight of his body on mine. Deep in my abdomen, heat began to rise, although my skin was cool against the tiled wall as I slid down. My fingers sought out the hot place and I began to stroke myself, remembering the sensation of Ewan's tongue on my inner thighs and his fingers pressing deeper. I laid my head back against the wall and closed my eyes, surrendering to the memory and to my own touch. The contrast of heat within and cold floor without enhanced the pleasure I was giving myself and I came quickly, slumping down against the side of the bath as my breathing slowed.

After a time I noticed it was quite dark, and took myself off to bed. My own, alone, lonely bed. I lay on it and thought some more. It gradually dawned on me that Ewan might not see our mutual experience in the same light as I did. Perhaps he saw it as an opportunity grasped. My inner voice said: "Maybe he's been playing you since day one, and now he's had what he was after?" No, I don't accept that. We were friends!

Could it be that what had felt to me like a seamless symphony of mutual understanding and responsiveness was only the dance of the human animal with its mate? Less than that, even. Not a mate: just chance-met partners. I cried a little in self-pity, but my mind was still working on the problem. I had to forge a new vision of relationships if I was going to survive being single.

I had married Drew for life, mistaking lust for love, but still believing I would receive in return pleasure and protection. That had been foolish. However, I had embraced Ewan just as unrealistically, assuming that since he gave me physical pleasure he must therefore want to engage with me permanently. Maybe I'd been naive, but I didn't want to accept that I was wrong. Some deeply romantic layer at my core still held the firm belief that pleasure of the degree I'd shared with Ewan must mean we were essentially compatible in other aspects of our lives. (It has to be true. Doesn't it?)

I slept poorly, and gave up altogether at around 5 a.m., taking myself off downstairs to make a cup of tea, and then abandoning it in favour of a good run. Four vigorous miles later I fell back in the door, ready for a quick shower and change of clothes. It occurred to me briefly that I hadn't run since The Day with Ewan, but I let the thought drift by unacknowledged. Then I reflected that starting this early on Mull meant it was still a respectable time in the evening in New Zealand. No sooner had the thought begun to form than I was dialling my grandparents' number.

"Hello?"

"Hello, Nanna. It's Cas."

"Hello, dear. It seems a long time since I heard your voice."

"It is. I always mean to phone, but then somehow the time slips away. How are you, Nanna?"

"I'm fine dear. Just a bit tired. You know how it is."

"What have you been up to lately?"

"Well, you know the cat under the barn had kittens?"

"I didn't know that. I thought the cat under the barn was a tom."

"No, not that one. The tortoiseshell. I don't know if that tabby tomcat is still around. Anyway, she had kittens. Your Granddad is letting me keep two of them. There's a wee ginger tomkit and a tortie female. But I can't think of names for them. Why don't you name them?"

"Oh. That's a lovely idea, Nanna. Can you give me a bit of time to think about it?"

"Of course I can. I expect you're quite busy."

"Yes. Sam's home for the holiday. He's not here right now, but he sends his love."

"That's nice, dear. Shall I call your Grandfather? Archie? Archie, it's Sandy." I heard the clunk as she set the phone down on the hall table. A few moments later she was back. "He isn't answering." Her voice was petulant.

I bit back the comment I wanted to make. I've called myself Cas since I was old enough to make up my own mind about my name. Most of the people who know me now are probably not

146

aware it's short for Cassandra, and only my grandparents still call me Sandy. There wasn't any point in revisiting that old argument.

"How is Granddad?"

"He's very busy, dear. Too busy to talk at the moment."

"What's he doing?"

"He has to supervise those boys on the roof. They're doing a good job up there, but they eat so many sandwiches. I hardly have time to myself these days."

"So, you're getting a new roof? Granddad's been complaining about it for long enough. He always says it will cost too much. Or are you only getting it fixed up?"

"New roof, dear. The rental's paying for it. Granddad is very pleased about it."

"Rental?"

"Your grandfather has rented the hill pastures to our new neighbour. Lovely man. I can't remember what his name is, now. Something Scottish, isn't it? Oh, I don't know. Anyway, he's got a lot of sheep, so he was happy to get more hill pastures. It's not so easy for your Granddad to get up there anymore."

"I can understand that. How about you? Are you well?"

"Yes, getting on very well indeed. My marmalade won the prize at the show. That's because I made it to my grandmother's secret recipe. You know my secret recipe?"

Her voice was sly, amused. She obviously felt she'd got one over me.

"No, I don't. You wouldn't tell me. You said it was a secret."

"It is a secret. Only the family women know."

"I'm family, Nanna. Remember."

"Oh, yes. Of course, dear. Here he is now. Archie? Archie, it's for you."

"Hello?"

"Hello Granddad, it's Cas. How are you?"

"Very well. All the better for hearing your voice. How are you? How's that grandson of mine?"

"We're both fine. Sam's doing well. He's got a job, just for the holidays, so he's not home at the moment."

"Good. That's what a young man needs – plenty of work to keep him out of mischief."

"Nanna said you were getting a new roof on."

"Yes, indeed. Only on the main house. It's needed it for a while. I rented the hill pastures to Collie. Good man. You remember him?"

"No, Granddad. I don't think I've ever met him."

"Really? I could have sworn…oh, well, never mind. Now, tell me, what mischief has that young rascal Sam been getting up to?"

I laughed to myself at the thought of Sam's big news. I'd have to find something else to tell them, though. I wasn't about to break his confidence.

"He's working as galley slave on a tourist boat," I said. "One of my friends offered him the work. He's doing really well at school, too. Especially in Maths." My voice broke slightly on the last word, but I don't think Granddad noticed.

"How are you for money, my girl? You know if you're ever in need you can come to us."

"I'm absolutely fine, Granddad. Everything's okay."

"Tell Sam when he finishes school he should come over for some work experience on the farm, while he works out what he's going to do next. I could put him up with Collie. He reckons there's a future in native timber, if you can wait for the return. He's putting his marginal land into rewarewa and mixed timber, in the hopes that the third generation will reap the profits. Now, that's what I call a long-term view."

That was interesting. It would take a convincing argument to win over my hard-working but conservative grandfather to any new land-use scheme. "So he's putting his own land into forestry, and renting your hill pastures?" I asked.

"Yeah. A good man. Hard-working." High praise indeed, from Granddad.

"It's a gap year, by the way."

"What was that?"

"They call it a gap year. When someone finishes school and then works for a year before going on to university."

"Does he really think he'll go on to university? He'll be the first in our family, you know."

I didn't remind him that I had a degree. Somehow, getting it part-time later in life wasn't quite the same. If Sam did go on to university, we could all be justly proud of him, without comparing him to anyone else.

"Oh, one more bit of news. My friend Bernadette just had a baby."

"That is good news. Hold on, Jenny's talking to me." I stopped talking. I could hear Nanna in the background, and Granddad's reply. "Jenny, Sandy's friend had a baby." Then he was back on the phone. "What was it, a boy or a girl?"

"A little girl called Emma Jane. Nine pounds two ounces."

"That's not so little. Is your friend all right? Did it all go well?"

"Yes, she's fine. She had no trouble at all."

"That's good. What about you? Anyone new in your life?"

"Leave it out, Granddad, I've only been divorced for six months. Anyway, the Isle of Mull isn't exactly bachelor central."

"All right, no need to get upset. We just worry about you. It would do us good to hear that you've settled down again. No, Jenny, it's all right. She's not really upset." Nanna's voice was audible in the background again, insistent. "Here you are then."

"Sandy, it's Nanna."

"Hello, Nanna."

"Now I want you to come home. It's no good you living in that strange place, so far away from your family. It really is time you came home again."

"I know. I wish I could. Maybe next year."

"All right, dear. Do you want me to put your grandfather back on again?"

"No, that's all right. Give him a kiss from me, won't you?"

"Of course I will. Don't forget to give me names for my cats."

"I'll call you as soon as I think of some."

"Bye, Sandy. Take care."

"Bye, Nanna. Love you."

I ended the call feeling much calmer and happier about myself, and greatly relieved about my grandparents. They sounded fine, and were obviously still enjoying life. As I walked about the room reviewing the call, I gradually realised they had told me nothing about their own health and wellbeing. Perhaps out of a sense that they didn't want to burden me with the problems of their old age? Or maybe because things were not as good as they should be, and they didn't want me to worry?

I did worry. I couldn't call them again tonight – would have to leave it at least a week, or they would start to think there was something I wasn't telling them, as indeed there was. I would just have to hope for the best, and add my grandparents to the list of people I was trying not to worry about. I moped about the house for most of the day, vaguely disturbed by something that was trying to come into my mind, but couldn't find space with all the worries I was trying not to have. Mid-afternoon I packed up a bag with some sandwiches and a flask, and took myself off in the car. I needed fresh air with a vengeance, and a short drive later I pulled up in the car park at Calgary Bay.

I turned away from the moderately populated sands and headed towards the old pier. It was a calming walk, between the cobalt sea on my left and the high talus slopes to my right. As I wandered along I caught a glimpse of an otter, just its rudder and back as it dived. I watched for a moment, but it didn't come up again. I felt a friendly warmth toward the otter and recalled that earlier sighting, the day Sam and I had gone to Oban with the chess queen.

Strange to think how much had happened since then: meeting Niall, and identifying the chess piece as authentic;

Sam's revelation about his sexuality; my own headlong dive into sex, and its confusing aftermath. Life went on, much the same. Calgary Bay was still beautiful and wild; the otters lived their own quiet, mysterious lives right under the noses of tourists and locals alike. The salt wind whipped at my hair, and I tucked strands of it behind my ears, stopping to gaze at the scenery while I thought.

Directly ahead, the path veered northeast, to bypass the great stone mass of An Sean Chaisteal, The Old Castle. This soaring peak, the remains of a great outpouring of volcanic rock erupted 50 million years before, dominated the coastline. On an impulse, I turned aside from the path and began to climb the rock.

After the first few metres of steep rock face, I found myself on a path of sorts. At first I assumed it was a sheep path, but as it meandered around the bulk of the rock into a little valley I passed the remnants of tiny stone houses, glimpsed between the trees of a small plantation of pines and spruce. Some of the inhabitants may have been removed from the land during the clearances, but it's probably not the whole story. Many are the reasons the villages of Mull lie empty and roofless.

I trudged on, and found myself climbing again. Eventually I hauled out at the top of another steep scramble, and stopped to catch my breath. Catch it I did: the view was spectacular. Far below me to the left, like a nail paring, lay the white crescent of Calgary Bay. To my right, and stretching away eastward, the orderly terraces of tertiary basalt that make up the bulk of northern Mull, but ahead of me, to the north, lay a precipitous descent into a rocky valley, dissected by streams.

Patches of bracken and flowering heather alternated with wind-shaped hazel groves, ending eventually in the hard line of a conifer plantation. Dead ahead as the sea bird flies the coastline was indented by another pale white paring. The hazel scrub ended at a terrace well above the high tide line, and the line of that terrace was marked with the unmistakeable pattern

151

of feannagan: the ridge and furrow of a village cultivation system. The on-and-off-again path appeared and disappeared between the patches of vegetation, but its scrappy line definitely led in the direction of that area of abandoned cultivation.

I sat and panted, my heartbeat drumming in my ears, gazing at the thin sliver of sand in the distance, and the blue and white and dark patterns of depth and current in the ocean beyond. I watched, mesmerised, as the sun flashed on distant water, and my eye was led out from the land into the sea channels, and from there around the jut of the headland and in again to the calm patch of turquoise lying off Calgary.

Slowly, as I watched the random patches of light and shade on the surface of the sea, events and experiences of the last few months began to come together in my mind, and a new pattern emerged. Without taking my eyes off the distant ocean, I felt in my pocket for my mobile phone. Miraculously, I was able to get a signal, and without looking at it I keyed in my own number. At the sound of my voice on the answer phone, I left a message for Sam. It was unlikely he'd ever hear it. Probably before he returned from his voyage I would be home, and the message erased. But better safe than sorry.

Shoving the phone back into my pocket, I turned slightly to give myself a better line of descent, and began to make my way down.

An hour of hard scrambling brought me down to the level of the cultivation ridges. Once I was walking among them, they were visible only as slight differences in ground level, although the pattern of ridge and furrow was still shown by patches of nettles, and the tendency of bracken to grow more lushly on top of the ridges. The low ground between the ridges was slushy with water. It was easy to see the value of the feannagan method: only the ridges, raised above the water table, would reliably grow crops year after year.

I waded through the bracken, aiming for the coast, and came out through a little hazel grove to the kind of view beloved by tourists and artists alike: ahead and a little below me, the white-sand beach stretched away, bounded by marram, the sand-binding grass, and other wild plants.

The tiny patch of machair edging the beach was rich with grass plumes and wild flowers; it seemed as though the sheep and rabbits hadn't found this spot. A low sand-cliff marked the high spring tide line around most of the beach, but I stood on an outcrop of sea-weathered basalt that jutted higher than the adjacent machair – it gave me a good overview of the site. I reached for my mobile and sent another quick message to my home phone.

The sound of water caught my ear and I looked across the machair towards a small stream, making its way down to the sea along the far edge of the beach. In a strange way, it reminded me of Huna Cove: the same configuration of rock, stream and sand, although my beloved secret bay was backed by that high, forest-covered cliff, which discouraged casual discovery.

This little beach was protected by its distance from the road system of Mull: now the sea-road was no longer the main means of travel, this sheltered cove had become completely isolated. I craned my neck to see if there were any signs of house sites in the machair, or on the bracken slopes behind it. I shuffled about, trying to see through the thin branches of the trees that edged the rock. As I moved sideways, my foot came down onto nothing: I lost my balance as my body lurched outward, and frantically grabbed at a branch as I fell. I heard a crack and a wild cry, and then nothing. Nothing at all for a very long time.

19

My feet skidded on the lino as I was shoved backwards. I pushed back and tried to twist out of his grasp, but his grip on my arms was too strong.

"Drew, let go. You're hurting me."

"I won't be spoken to like that in my own house." He leaned forward, using his superior weight and height to force me back towards the dark doorway.

"I didn't mean to upset you." That was a lie. He'd been niggling at me all evening: finding fault, apportioning blame. Putting me down in front of our son. Once Sam was safely tucked into bed I'd laid into him.

"Look, I don't care what sort of day you had at work; you can't come home and attack me to make yourself feel better. Pull yourself together and act like a man." I suppose I had only myself to blame. Looking back, I could see I'd chosen altogether the wrong set of words to use. Now he was behaving like a man – the way he thought a man should behave.

I raised my head and met his eyes, hoping I could make some kind of connection. We'd had our disagreements before. I'd tolerated several years of emotional and verbal abuse since my hasty, too-young marriage to the man of my dreams. But he hadn't physically harmed me in years. His blank eyes stared through me, his face emotionless, giving no outward sign of the rage consuming him.

I'd seen that look before – turned on the maid who spilled soup on his lap, the chauffeur who'd closed the door too sharply and caught Drew's tie in the jamb. A twist of fury would cross his face, and then it would go blank and empty. In those cases, he would whirl away, leave the room; to return minutes later,

154

calm and quiet, and go on with his day as if nothing had happened. Later, one would find the smashed cabinet, the hole in the wall. It wasn't done to assault employees: they might sue.

My lot was more normally a battery of words, put-downs and accusations. I was too low in his estimation to warrant physical chastisement. I'd long since learned not to fight back.

Today had been different. Today I'd been up to the university to sign on for a Science course. Today was the eve of my son's departure to boarding school. My last day as a stay-at-home Mum: tomorrow I'd say goodbye to my child, having lost the battle to keep him out of the family's traditional form of education. Today was the last day of my marriage, although Drew didn't know it yet.

I'd made a simple but devastating mistake; I'd forgotten that it was still today, and tomorrow was a long way off. In my words, and in their delivery, I'd allowed my contempt for Drew to surface, for one, fatal moment. In that moment, he'd broken. I watched the icy veil of anger descend over his features, and I saw him recognise, on some deep, subconscious level, that I'd moved to a new level of defiance. Horrified, I realised I'd brought this on myself.

The cellar door yawning behind me, I made a last attempt to struggle free. Drew smashed my shoulder against the doorpost, then lifted me bodily and thrust me through the opening. I staggered as my heels skidded over the edge of the first step. He went with me, pushing me downwards, scraping my shins against the step. I grabbed at his shirtfront to save myself and he let go my arms and, raising his upwards, brought them down against my grasping hands, breaking my grip. I teetered on the edge of the stairwell, but a frantic lunge for the banister stopped me from toppling backwards. The light faded out of the room as he pushed the door shut, and I heard the bolt slam home on the other side.

My eyes adjusted slowly to the blackness, but still I could see nothing, apart from a thin line of light marking the bottom of the door. I crept back up the stairs and knelt with my head pressed against the door.

"Drew? Drew, are you still there? I'm sorry. You're right. I shouldn't have spoken like that. Can we talk about it?"

"You can come out when you've learned your lesson." The vindictive hiss of his voice came clearly through the heavy door.

Silence. For a long moment. Then I heard the sound of his footsteps, moving away.

"Wait, come back! Let me out!" I shouted until my throat began to hurt. I cried for a long while. I went back over the events of the evening, identifying the points at which, if I'd backed down or said the right thing sooner, I might have been able to prevent this.

I nursed my wounds. I even slept, although I woke feeling stiff and not at all rested. It was still dark. I opened my eyes, and the darkness pressed on my eyeballs. I forced them wider, trying to make out something, anything at all in my surroundings. I forced myself to stay calm. The rapid thudding of my pulse in my ears was so loud that I couldn't hear anything from outside. For all I knew he was standing there, enjoying my fear. Somehow, I had to get through to him. I reached again for the locked door that held me prisoner.

For a moment, I was disorientated. Instead of the hard line of the step under my knees, I lay half-crouched on rough rock. It was cold against my cheek, and my fingers were scraped and sore. The ache of bruises on my legs and the sharp sting of abrasions were overlain with a single locus of pain in my arm. My legs were cold – and wet. At some point, while I was dreaming, water had soaked my lower limbs. With that, I began to remember.

I'd fallen from the rock. Into the rock? I reached out again, trying to make sense of my surroundings. Particles of grit slid under my fingers as I tried to move, and instantly pain flared in my arm. I gasped for breath, feeling my heart race as the pain peaked and slowly subsided. There was something very wrong there.

So – I had fallen. Injured myself. It was night. I thought about that. I'd reached the little cove at around three in the afternoon, so for it to be dark now I must have lain unconscious for several hours. I fought down a sudden fear of the darkness. This was no lightless cellar. I was not locked in. There was a sensible explanation for what had happened to me, and I needed to work out what it was. My head throbbed in sympathy with the pain in my arm. Working things out suddenly seemed like far too much work.

I'd been dreaming about things that had happened more than a decade ago: Sam's last night at home before starting school. I'd battered myself against the doorway, again and again, refusing to accept that I couldn't find a way out. In between attempts to force the door, while I regained my strength, I made plans. I was going to get out of here. If I didn't manage it by myself, someone would be bound to let me out in the morning. If I wasn't there for him, Sam would come looking for me. He'd let me out. I'd send him for his school bag, already packed and ready, while I ran for my wallet, passport and car keys. We wouldn't take much. The important thing was to get away quickly, before Drew realised what was happening. I knew we'd only get one chance.

If Sam didn't come, the maid was sure to come by at first light. Someone would come past, eventually. It might even be him. But I couldn't wait for that. I forced myself to go down the stairs, feeling my way, one step at a time, running my hands along the wall, trying to find the light switch. I tried to remember the layout of the basement. Was there a shelf or a cupboard with a torch in it? I tried to force myself to move away from the bottom step, into the darkness, but I couldn't make the move. In the end, I had to admit that the light switch for the cellar was on the outside of the locked door; and that the door at the top of the stair was the only way out.

I crept back up the stairs, nursing my bruises, and crouched again, feeling with my fingertips for the gap under the door, willing my eyes to glimpse the faintest hint of light. I couldn't think of anything else to try. This time, I really was helpless. Eventually, I fell asleep again.

I came awake from a black nothingness, screaming as I clutched at my arm. I panted shallowly, feeling the blood pound in my temples in time to the throbbing on my left – my whole arm from the shoulder downwards alive with pain and heat. Still only half-conscious, I rolled away from it, somehow believing I could move myself away from the source of pain. The pain was like an animal, gnawing at my arm, and the more I moved the more it hurt me.

Forcing myself to stay still, I concentrated on my breathing, trying to drive the pain down to a manageable level. An endless dim corridor of time passed, during which I must have swum in and out of consciousness, listening to the endless litany of hate from my ex-husband. ("Stupid woman. What a waste of space you are. I don't know why I bother with you".)

Sometimes the distant, shushing roar of the sea seemed closer, and as the long night wore on a cold finger of wind reached into the place where I lay confined, and ran its fingers through my saturated clothing. Shivering caused spikes of pain from my injured arm, and I tried to force myself to lie still. Eventually, the breeze dropped and the shivering diminished. I even managed to sleep for a while, although my rest was troubled with half-remembered dreams and night terrors. I woke from one dream clinging to the rough rock of my enclosure, scouring the skin from my fingertips as I dug them into the stone. Slowly I came back to myself and began to take stock.

As I began to feel calmer, I ran my fingers as gently as possible up the injured arm, finding with relief that I still had all my fingers, and an intact elbow, although I could hardly bear to touch it. Further up I could feel the edge of the bulge where the broken bone pressed against the skin, trying to get out. I whimpered at that point and lost awareness for a while, as fear and pain flooded in. Later I remember wedging myself into the tiny rockbound space, trying to find a position where I could endure interminable hours of darkness as I drifted into sleep.

Once I woke to feel waves lapping against my body and, in trying to wriggle further into shelter, nudged the injured arm. The flare of pain knocked me away again. Another time I was sure I could almost see a star, my head twisted round to stare straight up into the solid rock ceiling above me, but it was definitely there. Star light, star bright, wishing fiercely for Sam, even though I knew he was safe away at sea on Ewan's boat. How can I see a star if there's rock above me? Maybe this is what they mean about seeing stars. Did I hit my head as well as my arm?

Later I roused to a red flare of pain that drove everything else from my mind except the senseless compulsion to endure without crying out – as if once to complain aloud would open the floodgates to hysteria or madness. At last, a tiny moan forced itself between my gritted teeth, and I clenched my jaw harder, releasing a wave of pain that took me back into the black waters of unconsciousness.

I dreamed that I was drowning. Inky waters, thick as mud, poured into my throat and lungs, their density dragging me downward into the dark. I dreamed I was trapped under a landslide – buried alive under tons of rubble, trying to cry out so that I would be rescued. But my throat would make no sound.

I dreamed that I flew: not my usual dream of flying, where I frantically flapped my arms and inched through the air, trying to gain enough height to avoid power lines, or lunging monsters. This time I soared high into the ionosphere, with stars around me, and plunged through clouds into a blue sea: plummeting like Icarus from the terrible heat that had burnt my wings, my arms. Thin black bones stuck out from my shoulders and I had no hands – no hands to break my fall!

Again and again I relived the darkness of the cellar – breaking my fingernails on the door that wouldn't open. I saw, clear in my memory despite the utter blackness of my surroundings, the white, shocked face of my son, staring out of the back window of the car as he was driven away. My hands clenched, desperate to reach for my child, and my eyes ached with the tears that would no longer fall. The sea muttered in the distance, and I began to hear voices.

20

The pain in my left arm had gone far away, although as I shifted position it threatened to come in close again. I lay still until it receded, then opened my eyes. For a moment, I closed them again: bright fluorescence against a white ceiling caused a throb of pain in my temples, but as I blinked my pupils adjusted and my head cleared. I raised it carefully from the pillow and tried to work out where I was. I lay on a metal bed under a lurid turquoise cover, in a white room that smelled of lemons, disinfectant and complex cooking odours, not entirely unpleasant. The unmistakable aroma of hospital.

I shifted again, ignoring the dull thud of pain from my upper arm, and looked around the room. A four-bed ward, although only one other bed was occupied – by a turquoise-shrouded lump that I hoped was simply asleep. As I tried to focus on my surroundings, unconnected bubbles of memory rose and burst onto the surface of my mind. Sam's face, streaked with dirt and tears. The orange glow of the lifeboat men in their matching jackets, gently joking in calm voices as they hauled my stretcher-bound body. Some feeble remark from me about the lengths to which one has to go to get the attention of men. And again my own voice, in a dark place that smelled of brine and rot: a thin, small, frightened voice, saying "Ewan?"

I closed my eyes again and tried to piece it together. Moving restlessly, I became aware that the heaviness of my left arm was caused by a plaster cast, encasing it from wrist to shoulder. That realisation triggered the memory of a sickening plunge into blackness, and with it almost the whole experience flooded back.

I remembered falling. The details were still hazy, but I'd

endured a long time lying on rock, with a broken arm. Long enough for the tide to come in at least twice, soaking my legs and feet. Long enough for thirst and pain to drive me down into the darkness in the back of my mind: the dark place I avoid, inhabited by my personal demons, all of which speak in my ex-husband's carefully modulated, oh-so-calm voice. Such sensible, reasonable sounding comments: I was the one with the problem, after all. Drew's voice nagged on in the back of my head, and somehow I knew I'd been hearing all those complaints and comments, even deep in unconsciousness.

"I don't need to hit a woman to control her."

"Why would I waste another moment of my life discussing this, or any, subject with you?"

When I had finally made it home from the hospital, with a six-week-old baby smaller than a newborn – a child I hardly knew, who cried day and night and seemed to suffer from permanent colic – I'd been a wreck. I wasn't sleeping, the baby never slept, and each day seemed longer than the last.

I begged Drew for help, but he told me it was my job to manage. "How useless are you? This is what you wanted: all women are made to be mothers. You're the only one who can't do it. There must be something seriously wrong with you."

Until, one night, I lay full length on the floor: the baby finally, miraculously, sleeping, but so confused by depression and broken nights that I couldn't sleep myself. I was rhythmically hitting my head on the doorpost. In some muddled-up way, I perceived the pain as comforting. Drew lay next to me, whispering. "He doesn't need you. He'd be better off without you. The planet would be a better place without you in it. You know what you need to do." On and on, while I lay silently rocking. Inside my head, I raged at him, anything to make him shut up, but the words were dammed up behind my closed mouth. If only he would help me. It would be enough if he would just hold me, and let me cry…and sleep.

Later, he came back down the stairs and stopped next to

where I lay, in the grey limbo between sleep and unconsciousness. I felt a booted foot stir my ribs. When I didn't respond, the foot kicked again, harder. I couldn't summon up the energy for confrontation – it just didn't seem to matter anymore. He grunted, a sound of pure contempt. Then he crossed over my prone body, heel grinding into the small of my back. His weight pressed me down into the hard, stone floor and he walked away. Neither of us had spoken a word.

Somehow, in the misery of my sojourn under the rock, my half-conscious mind had chosen to revive my least favourite memories. Injury, shock and exposure had made me relive some of the worst moments of my marriage. Those experiences had made me stronger, though. I never let Drew lock me in the cellar again. From that moment, I'd known what he was capable of, if pushed. I woke to a thin line of grey light under my fingers, and when I pushed the door it opened.

I hadn't waited to learn who had released me; I ran for my room, my purse and car keys. When I got there, I heard the gates opening. I reached the window just in time to see the small figure of my son, heavy backpack on his narrow shoulders, walking away. Drew climbed into the front seat and the car headed out of the driveway.

Sam's white face was in the rear window, staring back towards the house. I banged on the glass but, of course, he couldn't hear me. Drew took him away from me, and he became the hostage for my good behaviour. So long as I toed the line, I was permitted to see him, on the occasions when he came home from school.

I stayed in the marriage, although I railed at myself for cowardice. If I wanted to see Sam, I had to meet Drew's exacting and petty requirements. I had no doubt that at any point, for no reason other than the pleasure he derived from tormenting me, Drew could take Sam away, and I would never see him again.

No wonder I'd relived that horrible time. Physical pain and

lonely terror had unlocked the door to a memory I'd tried to forget. No wonder I'd run away from it again – all the way into unconsciousness.

Much later I swam back from the abyss, just a little way. I dreamed I stood knee-deep in foam, clutching a fish-spear: feeling with my toes for the subtle movement of flatfish, tasting already the creamy grilled flesh. I licked the salt from dry lips, constantly trying to draw moisture out of my mouth. The unstable surface roiled beneath my feet and I stumbled deeper into the water, hearing in the noise of tumbled foam a voice – a call I had to turn to. Deep in the dark, I strained toward that voice: perhaps the only voice that could have brought me back. "Sam," I whispered.

This time the artificial brightness of the light was unsurprising, though no less painful. I squinted at the figure leaning over me. Sam's concerned face swam into view, and I reached my right arm to him. He took it and grinned with relief. "Hi, Mum," he said.

A glass of water and a dose of painkillers later, I sat propped up on pillows and interrogated my son. "What on earth were you doing there? Thank goodness you came, but how? When did you get back from Tiree?" And, in a burst of fear, "What's the date?"

"Don't worry, Mum. It was only the day before yesterday that you fell down your pit. We got you out of there the next night, and the lifeboat brought you over to Oban. They said you were dehydrated and had a broken arm, but otherwise only cuts and bruises. You were lucky."

"Don't I know it," I said fervently, recalling my first waking, and the closeness of the sea to the ledge on which I had lain. "But what happened to your trip to Tiree?"

"Oh, well, it all went pear-shaped. We got on the boat alright, and headed off to Tobermory for the pick-up. But when we reached there, Ewan got a message that the people had cancelled. They'd paid in advance, so he's not unhappy, and we picked up a taxi run to Coll instead. But it meant we got back two days earlier than expected. Ewan ran me home, and kept on driving: a mate of his called him to go out fishing for a few days, so he was going straight to the ferry. I listened to your message as soon as I got in."

I recalled my frightened voice in the dark, calling Ewan's name in relief, and the strong arm and shoulder that had supported and comforted me as I waited for the stretcher to be lowered down. A person who had rappelled confidently down a hanging rope into my prison, and swiftly reported to the men waiting above. I had leaned on that confidence, secure in the knowledge that my man had come to rescue me. I had been only semi-conscious, and hardly making sense, but I recalled an embarrassingly intimate level of dependence on that person – that stranger?

"Who came down the rope, then?"

"That was an amazing coincidence. I got your messages as soon as I came in, and I started worrying because you weren't back. But the next message on the machine was from Niall. He'd been doing some thinking, and background research. He even knew about the thing Ewan's grandfather had found. He said he was coming over to check an area – and it was exactly the same area you'd given in your second message.

"I rang him up, and he came over straight away. He had this fast motorboat – a RIB – and he picked me up at the head of Loch Cuin, by Dervaig. We zoomed around the coast like James Bond, and came into the little cove, straight up onto the sand. We wandered about calling your name, until I heard you under the rocks. It was Niall who called the coastguard for help, and then fixed the ropes and got down to you. He was fantastic!"

"Niall," I said faintly. I sent my awareness back into the dark and had to agree. That sense of comforting familiarity had been no illusion; but rather than the absent lover, the man on whom I had leaned had turned out to be a recent acquaintance, albeit one about whom I had entertained some fairly intimate fantasies. I blushed, and turned my head on the pillow, but fortunately Sam wasn't paying attention.

Niall made more sense, the more I thought of it. I could remember trying to come to my feet with his support, leaning on the black bank beneath which I had sheltered. In the light of his helmet-torch, I had seen a red-brown stain on my palm, which puzzled me: the hand was not injured, and the stain would not rub off.

"What's that," I had asked, pathetically, holding out the hand.

"That's a rivet, my dear."

The supporting arms had become even more gentle and tender, as if I, or something about me, had suddenly become very precious.

A disturbance of voices outside the room heralded the arrival of another visitor. Sam got up and, relinquishing my hand, headed for the door. My view of the nurses' station was obscured by a partly-drawn bed-curtain, and I waited with mild curiosity as I heard Sam's voice join the low murmur. After a moment, footsteps approached, and Sam appeared round the curtain with Niall Webster.

I blushed again furiously, but Niall was still speaking with Sam and didn't notice. He looked down at me and held out a bunch of carnations and gypsophila: "I was going to bring chocolates," he said, "but Sam told me you don't like them." Sam grinned over Niall's shoulder, and produced a large box of chocolates from behind his back. "I'm saving you from fat and spots," he sniggered.

I gave a mock howl of outrage, and grabbed for the chocolates – simultaneously, my arm gave a throb of pain, Niall started in surprise and Sam dropped the chocolates. In the ensuing scramble, I got my equilibrium back and Niall wrestled Sam for the chocs. Gaining control, he pulled off the ribbon and presented the open box to me while I giggled foolishly.

A disapproving face put itself round the curtain and scolded in a whisper: we were disturbing the rest of the ward.

"That was your fault," whispered Sam as the face withdrew.

"Yours," muttered Niall, childishly. They scowled at one another, then both laughed. I marvelled at the easy companionability of my knights-in-armour: having rescued the damsel in distress, they were male-bonding in earnest.

Niall sent Sam off to the patients' lounge with three individual coffee-makers which he'd had in his backpack ("hospital coffee is always horrible") and settled himself in the armchair next to my bed.

"Um…thanks for everything," I said. Niall said nothing. He was not ill at ease, but simply seemed to dismiss his part in my rescue as irrelevant. I waited a moment, and then went on:

"Niall, what were you doing there?"

This time he grinned in real excitement, and pulled out a pile of newspapers from under the bed. As he brandished the top copy, I could read the headline:

'Mull Woman Makes Historic Find.'

I settled back on my pillows as Niall began to read: "*Mull resident Cassandra Longmore was out walking her dog two days ago when she fell off a cliff, injuring herself seriously. When rescued, she was found to be lying inside a cavern, partly excavated by the sea…*"

I snorted, and Niall stopped reading. "It's not a very accurate account," he admitted, "but you were hardly available to give interviews. However, the gist of it is correct: you, Cassandra Longmore, have made the archaeological find of my career, let alone the island, the country or the century. At this minute you are absolutely my favourite person!"

"Oi," said Sam, coming in with the coffees. "What about me?"

"I couldn't have done it without you," said Niall.

"Done what?" I demanded. "I'm fed up with waiting for someone to make sense. All I did was to fall down a hole when I was trying to be clever."

"Ah, but that wasn't just any hole. The same sea that had been working away at the cliff edge, and had opened the blowhole you fell into, had also been excavating an artificial construct: an earth-filled cavern shaped by the decay of an upturned boat. A boat that was probably buried at least 800 years ago."

I blinked in astonishment. "A boat burial. That's what you're talking about, isn't it?"

"Well," Niall hedged. "It may be a deliberate burial, or it may be a boat-hull used as a house that became buried naturally following abandonment, or even an upturned boat washed in on a very high tide and gradually covered over. But my money's on a burial. It would be a first for Mull if it is."

"Would that mean better publicity for you and AIAS?" teased Sam, but Niall turned his most serious expression on him.

"I would never try to overstate the evidence," he said. "It will take a slow and careful excavation of the whole site before we can make any claim with confidence. However, we have found something I wanted you to see immediately."

He reached into his pocket and brought out a silk handkerchief, unrolling it to reveal a small plastic envelope almost completely covered by a large, white copiously-labelled sticker. He cradled it in his hand for a moment, then turned it round and held it up triumphantly before my face. In the envelope, shorn in half across the waist but unmistakeable, was the top part of a fierce, shield-biting warrior: a warder.

"It seems," said Niall happily, "that we've uncovered your queen's home. It would beggar belief for there to be two sites containing authentic chess pieces in this part of Mull. I believe your queen was washed out of the site at the last set of high spring tides, not long before you picked it up at Calgary Bay. It hadn't been in the sea long enough to be damaged by salt water. And I think the set of scales found by Ruairidh MacLean must also have come from this site. The ocean has been nibbling at its edges for a long time."

"I knew that!" I cried. "When I stood at the top of the hill and looked north toward that little bay, I suddenly thought I could see how the currents could carry stuff out of there and round the point into Calgary. Ewan told me his grandfather had found the mangled scales offshore from an abandoned village north-east of Calgary."

"Then you knew more than I did," said Niall. "Sam gave me that information, which led us straight to the right area. When he found you, we expected the worst, but it turned out your injury wasn't as bad as we feared. You were suffering from hypothermia, though. I wouldn't have liked to see you spend another night out there. Sam saved your life."

Sam looked sheepish as I reached for his hand again. "I know," I said softly, looking back in one overflowing instant at the whole of Sam's first sixteen years, from conception to near-adulthood: my beloved son. "I know."

21

The last few weeks have been very quiet, thank goodness. They let me go home after another night's observation, but it's taking me a long time to get back on top of things. Sam finished his Geography project: after all, I'd handed the story to him on a plate, and he exchanged a lot of emails with Niall who has given him an amazing amount of help.

Henry was as good as his word and sent me some non-scientific stuff to proofread. Actually, I think I prefer the Physics and Chemistry texts. There are only so many ways you can interpret a phrase in a scientific publication. My work rate has slowed. Working one-handed makes handling the printouts difficult, and I'm now a painfully slow two-finger typist, but I persevere and slowly my arm improves.

I got an infection, and they found the break wasn't healing, so I had to have it reamed out and re-plastered, and now I'm waiting to get the second plaster off and start rebuilding my strength. I haven't been running for weeks – even walking pounds my arm too much, and I've become a virtual recluse. Obviously I can't drive, and although the bus to Tobermory goes past the door, I find it difficult to carry more than a small bag of shopping back home. Sam didn't want to go back to school – he was worried I wouldn't be able to feed myself. So just before he was due to leave I went to see Ewan.

Ewan had been unaware of my little adventure until he got back from his fishing trip. Hector had saved the article from the Oban Times (as he told me later), so Ewan knew I'd been injured within a day or two of me leaving hospital. Did he get in touch? Did he hell.

I didn't bother to make contact with him at first. Every time

I thought about seeing him, I felt hurt and confused again. I couldn't decide what I wanted to do. If he wanted more from me than a one-night stand, surely he would keep in touch? Was he too shy? He is so reserved; I could well understand if he couldn't work out what to say.

If he didn't want more than we'd already shared – well, it was too late to decide that. Things will go forward one way or another, but what's done can't be undone. Probably he wished that human relationships could be arranged as wordlessly as animal ones. Surely if he cared, he would come round and offer to help? Or did he fear that any offer of assistance would be misconstrued? I got fed up with myself chewing over all the possibilities, again and again, getting nowhere. So I picked myself up, walked out in the August drizzle and went to Hector's place.

I'd been locked up in my den of misery for so long that I'd forgotten how lovely Mull can be in late summer. All around me, the fences and plants were coated with moisture, and the long grass of my garden gleamed with dew-laden cobwebs. I left the gate open, hoping that my garden nemeses, the sheep, would invite themselves in and mow it. It didn't seem likely I would be doing any serious gardening for many weeks to come. My arm ached and I rubbed my shoulder ruefully as I wandered down the road.

Autumn colour was already visible in the beech hedge. Beeches are far north of their natural range here – they'll grow on Mull, but they come into leaf late and die off early. The big oaks were barely on the turn, leaf edges browning but their centres still green. The ash tree that loomed over Ewan's caravan had lost all its leaves, though, and its bare branches were relieved only by a skinny rowan that had somehow survived long enough in its shade to put out a few clumps of orange berries. The drizzle gradually lifted as I walked, and a distant shaft of watery sun struck through to illuminate the mist-covered hills. A faint hint of rainbow hovered in its path as I opened the gate and went in to knock at Hector's door.

How nice it was to see the old man again. It seemed such a long time since I'd last sat there, with a belly full of mackerel, although in reality it had only been a few weeks.

"Cassandra," he said. "Madainn mhath a ghraidh. Thig a steach."

'Good morning and come in' is about the limit of my Gaelic. There have been visits when he and Ewan have conversed over my head, and I've barely caught one word in twenty. I suspect they do it when they don't want me to know they're arguing. One of these days I'm going to learn to speak the language, and that'll serve them right.

Hector sat me down in front of the fire, with Molly to warm my feet (what a weight that dog is – she's getting fat in her old age) and went off to make me a cup of tea. I felt a slight draught and turned my chair toward the fire, reaching out a foot to rub Molly's stomach.

Hector was away such a long time I was starting to worry, but eventually he turned up with a mug for each of us. "Damn boy," he muttered, and followed it up with a guttural phrase of Gaelic. I looked at him, but no further remark was forthcoming.

We sat and sipped in companionable silence. After a while, Hector began to talk.

"We've been lucky with the weather. Not too much rain."

"I know. I keep waiting to wake up to the cold and wet, but it seems as though summer is hanging on a bit longer this year."

"That damn fool dog. You'll never guess what she's been doing."

I shook my head. "Molly? I thought all she did these days was sleep."

"Won't stir for a rabbit, even when it runs across her foot. But she's decided to start chasing butterflies." He nudged Molly with his foot, and she raised her head and looked at him. Her tail thumped on the floorboards.

"She's left it a bit late for that hasn't she?"

"About the only thing still on the wing is the Scotch Argus. The lawn's full of them. It's the boy's fault. Hasn't been mowing it enough. It looks more like a hay meadow than a lawn."

The last thing I wanted was to start a session of mutual complaint about Ewan. "Sam's working hard. He's writing up a school project, all about the Calgary chess piece and the archaeological site on the coast. You know Ewan told me about the piece Ruairidh MacLean found?"

"Aye, that was Ellie's old man. He was a grumpy sod. Didn't think much of me, I can tell you. At one point I thought I might have to kidnap her: the old way."

"Kidnap her?"

"Yes, that was sometimes done. In those days a girl had to be very careful about being alone with a man. If rumours got round about her behaviour, he would be told he had to marry her. If he refused, she could be ruined, even if the rumours weren't true. So sometimes, if the father didn't agree to the marriage, the boy would kidnap the girl. That way she could say she was innocent, but the father would still have to agree to the match.

"I suppose it was an old-fashioned thing, even then. I don't know anyone who actually did it. She told her father she was going to run away with me, and if he didn't like it she'd never be back to visit. He said he'd thrash the skin from her bones for speaking in such an insolent way to her Da, and she told him if he did she would go to church and tell everyone that she'd been with me.

"She was a wild girl, my Ealasaid. I wouldn't ever have wanted to cross her. She had a mean eye – yes, and a hard hand to go with it. She could sing, though. You've never heard anything more beautiful than that wee slip of a girl, singing to her bairn. It brought me home to her, of a night: wanting to be there, in the warm, dark house, listening to my wife singing to our son."

"You must miss her a lot."

Hector surreptitiously wiped a tear from the corner of his eye. "From time to time, I do. She's a long time gone, though. At times I look at her photograph and I can't quite bring her to mind. Still, it won't be long and I'll be joining her."

"Don't be daft. You're as strong as an ox, Hector. You'll see the lot of us off."

"More like well pickled," he said. "The amount of whisky I've put away over the years. She liked a tot, my Ellie. Nothing like whisky in your belly to settle marital problems."

He looked at me sideways. I held my breath. What was he getting at?

Hector rumbled to himself in Gaelic. Then he said, "The boy's at home. Go and see him, mo chridhe. He ought to talk to you."

"He's not much of a talker," I said ruefully.

"Make him."

Ruffling Molly's neck, I stood and let myself out. I crossed the lawn to the gate and took the path to Ewan's caravan. I knocked.

After a few minutes, I knocked again. The drizzle had deepened and a little trickle of water ran down the back of my neck. I pulled up my collar just as the door opened. Ewan stood there. "Better come in," he said.

In I went. I got another cup of tea. It's a good way to let tension dissipate and gives you something to hide behind too. I waited while he poured, not speaking. He was silent too.

Once he sat down, I hit him with it. "Ewan, I don't regret what we did. I hope you don't." I ploughed onward without giving him a chance to speak. "But things are difficult now. I need your help."

I paused. I wasn't sure quite what I was going to say next. Ewan cleared his throat and I waited for him to speak.

"I'm sorry…" the awkward pause dragged on.

"No, that's wrong. I'm not sorry. Not sorry at all. But…" His voice trailed off and he shuffled his feet, head down. I felt distressed, as much on his behalf as my own. I have never before seen this man look other than self-possessed.

"I'm afraid of spoiling our friendship." I ended the sentence on an upward note – a hint of a question.

"Yes." He nodded and took a great gulp of his tea.

"I want to suggest…well, can we put it behind us? I know we can't pretend it didn't happen, and I don't want to. But let's not make it be too important. If I'm out running in a few weeks, and I see you coming down the road with Molly, I want to be able to fall in beside you and just run the way we used to. We don't need to talk. Or you can let me do all the talking as usual."

Hmm. I think that was the hint of a smile. Ewan nodded again, and seemed a lot more comfortable. I rushed on before I lost my courage. "The trouble is that at the moment I can't drive and can't carry much, so my cupboards are getting bare. Sam doesn't want to go back to school and leave his crippled Mum to starve to death in her own home. When you get Hector his weekly supplies, could you get some stuff for me too? Just until I'm back on my feet. Before anything I need someone to go out to Calgary and bring back my car from the car park. Sam keeps threatening to go and do it himself."

"Yes. Of course. That's no trouble." (Wow, three sentences. He must be feeling better.) I smiled at Ewan and told him I had to go. In truth, I needed to get out of there before I confused myself any more. I was starting to feel like an experienced older woman who has taken advantage of a teenager, in utter contrast to the way I had felt on the day we'd made love, when it had seemed as if Ewan was in complete control.

If anything I was feeling more uncomfortable than before I'd started talking. But Ewan's body language was much more relaxed and I had to assume we'd mended our bridges, whatever that meant for the future.

Next morning, Ewan turned up at the door. Sam let him in.

"Hey," said Ewan, nodding to him companionably. "Taking good care of your Mum?"

"Yep. She has to do what I tell her or I won't let her scratch under the cast."

"Swine," I said, poking him with the knitting needle I was using for the job.

"I've come for your shopping list," said Ewan, handing Sam a bag with some milk, bread and plums in it. "Plums are from Dad," he added.

So that problem was solved. I think that, given time, we will find ourselves once more jogging peaceably together, as if nothing had ever happened. How peculiar life is.

As for my reawakened (or, for that matter, newly awakened) body: I have to live with it. It's not showing any signs of going back to sleep, although the problems with my arm have kept nicer feelings at bay. I've decided I shall cross that bridge when I come to it – and whether or not the bridge I mended with Ewan is the same bridge, I just don't know.

Niall I haven't seen. What news I get comes via Sam, and it's clear the boy has a new enthusiasm. If Archaeology was being offered at school, he'd definitely be studying it. Let's just say that, well…Space School is permanently off the menu. Sam went back to school full of the story of his adventure, and he has since told me he got top marks in his class for the story of the Calgary chess piece.

I miss him. After his moment of glory, rescuing me from certain death, things have become much calmer and more peaceful between us. I would have thought that seeing me down a hole in the dark - injured, useless and depending on him for help - would make him feel insecure. Instead, it has marked another milestone in his developing maturity.

I can see that next time he's here I will have to be incredibly well organised and totally in control, otherwise he's going to take over. In my early stages of recovery, he did everything. I didn't even know he could cook, let alone run a laundry and bathing schedule for a grumpy invalid. It's good to know he's going to be all right.

I've been calmer with him too; aware at last that I'm part of the problem. From the moment he arrived I was constantly tense, expecting a fight (and of course children give their parents what they are asking for). My fears seem a little silly now. Imagine: the worst I could come up with was that he had developed a secret drinking habit. Instead, he is still the sensible, level-headed, if anything too controlled, young adult he has been steadily becoming right in front of my eyes over the last few years. If anyone can chart the unknown waters of the future, it's Captain Samfast the Extraordinary.

He hasn't told his Dad about being gay. I've promised I won't say a word. That's Sam's story to tell. I did give him an enormous string of multi-coloured condoms. The look on his face when I pulled them out was priceless. He couldn't decide whether to be furious or amused. I'd even managed to source a brown paper bag to hide them in. At that, his outrage subsided and he laughed with me. I notice, however, that he managed to 'accidentally' leave them under his bed when he went back to school. I have a feeling that's not the last time Sam's going to have the last word.

22

Late in January, as one of the east coast's fierce winter storms lashed the capital, I found myself a guest of the Edinburgh Metropolitan Museum. Niall met me in Oban and drove me down, detouring to collect Sam from Waverley Station. The atmosphere in the car was subdued. The second stint in plaster, and my own bad behaviour in not keeping up with the physiotherapy exercises, meant that my arm was still not strong enough for driving. It was also prone to ache in cold weather, and I found myself concentrating so hard on not being unremittingly grumpy about it that I wasn't up to much in the way of conversation.

Sam too was unusually taciturn: immediately I began to worry that school was responsible. He'd grown up so much over the summer – had he found it difficult to go back into the rules-and-regulations environment of school? I was still finding it difficult to let go of my need to control Sam, especially with the extra worries he had given me to chew over, but Sam did not want to talk about it, whatever 'it' was, and in the end the silence was not uncomfortable.

Niall filled some of the conversational space by telling us what he'd managed to achieve so far at the site of my serendipitous accident. The short version is…not much. He'd gained permission to carry out a rescue dig, but the trouble was that there was so little to see, and access was proving a problem. He hadn't managed to get out to the site at all since the beginning of December, and had been forced to delay any further investigation until the weather improved in the spring.

The truncated warder he'd shown me in the hospital remained the star find, although he did say he believed he'd seen discolouration of the material in the floor of the space where I'd lain, and speculated that it might represent decayed bone. As for the 'rivet', even that identification was in doubt. His colleagues had pointed out that it might represent decay of a particularly iron-rich nodule in the basalt wall of the chamber. Given all these frustrations, he was remarkably cheerful about the site and remained convinced that eventually he would be able to work out exactly what had happened there.

Once in the museum, Niall led us to a room set out with the past year's discoveries from a range of digs across Scotland. AIAS had its own corner, where buttery glimmers of gold and splashes of bright ceramic were overshadowed by trays and cabinets full of brown chips of bone and shards of pottery: the real meat of archaeology.

There was a display there from the Islay dig, where Niall's colleagues had dissected a Mesolithic midden. The case seemed to hold vast numbers of shells, and a mound of hazel nuts. It was hard to imagine they represented anything other than basic food gathering practices, but alongside them were a handful of microliths: tiny pieces of flint, expertly knapped and retouched to act as perfect miniature tools. I couldn't get over how beautiful they were.

In pride of place, at the centre of the room, stood a cabinet holding three items: a crushed, almost shapeless piece of metal, carefully arranged to display the exquisite etching of a running dog; my queen, sitting calmly on her throne; and, standing before her, supported on a shaped Perspex block: the broken warder, once again fiercely guarding his sovereign.

I gazed at the stern figure of the warder and, from behind him, the Calgary queen regarded me with satisfaction. Two female protagonists: both had passed through storms to find safe anchorage. The queen retained one protector; she no longer had to face the future alone.

I shivered, perceiving empty depths that I hadn't plumbed yet. I comforted myself by wrapping my arms around the male shoulders on either side of me: the cosseted son and the new-found friend. For a moment it felt like completeness, and I gazed down again, entranced, at the little queen's smug expression, oblivious to what was happening around me.

The Calgary queen watched impassively as, behind the woman's back, one long-fingered hand reached out uncertainly, withdrew, then reached again until the slender fingers touched the other's wrist. That arm grew rigid a moment, then its owner moved slightly and his own hand came up to caress in turn. Soundlessly, two sets of fingers stretched and interlaced, gripping with fierce strength. Wordlessly, a connection was confirmed. The future began.

THE END

Author's Note

Cas Longmore lives on the Isle of Mull in Western Scotland. But then again, she doesn't. Her world is very like ours – an alternative Mull, just around the corner of reality from the world that you and I inhabit. Some places look the same on the map, but others are very different. One whole section of her Isle of Mull doesn't exist in our world, and other parts have altered their geography in subtle ways.

The same is true of the people: no one in this book resembles any real person, living or dead. They are like us in the ways that all humanity is similar, and as different as inhabitants of different universes can be. The history of Cas's Mull is very like the history of our own, but not exactly the same. Any mistakes are my own – I am not a perfect chronicler of her story – and should not be taken to reflect any reality that historians or geographers recognise in our own universe.

Wherever possible I have used real research and historical publications to keep me on track. If you are interested to read more on the subjects raised in the book, I have attached a partial bibliography, listing some of my sources. In particular, I would recommend Adam Nicolson's book '*Sea Room*', for a glimpse of the history of an island group in the Hebrides. In it you will find a real archaeological treasure, with a story every bit as mysterious as that of the Calgary chessman.

Glossary

Gaelic words and phrases

Birlinn: a wooden, clinker built ship which could be sailed or rowed, used off the west coast of Scotland from the Middle Ages onwards. The word and design are similar to Nordic vessels of the same period.

Faoileag: 'Seabird', especially various species of gull. It can also mean the white crest on a wave.

Feannagan: 'lazy beds'. The system of ridge and furrow cultivation, where planted ridges are raised above the peaty soil, built up by annual applications of seaweed and sand.

Madainn mhath a ghraidh. Thig a steach: Good morning, dear. Come in.

Mo chridhe: my heart, a term of endearment.

An Sean Chaisteal: the old castle.

Māori words

Huna: hidden, secret.

Pounamu: greenstone jade. Also used to denote an object as especially precious.

Rewarewa: *Knightia excelsa*. A fine-grained hardwood tree, native to New Zealand.

Scots words

Bairn: a baby.

Dreich: dreary, bleak.

Fank: a sheep enclosure.

Machair: fertile, low-lying grassy plain found on the western coasts of Scotland and Ireland.

Partial Bibliography

The Archaeology of Argyll, Edited by Graham Ritchie, Edinburgh University Press, 1997.

The Hebrides: A Natural Tapestry, J.M. Boyd and I.L. Boyd, Birlinn Ltd, 1996

A History of Scotland, Neil Oliver, Weidenfeld & Nicolson, 2009.

Island Voices, Traditions of North Mull, Ann MacKenzie, Birlinn Ltd, 2002

Investigating the Lewis Chess Pieces (Suil air Fir-Taileisg Leodhais), CD ROM, Trustees of the National Museums of Scotland, 1999.

The Kingdom of the Isles: Scotland's western seaboard, c1100 – c1336, R. Andrew McDonald, Birlinn Ltd, 2008.

The Kingdom of Scotland in the Middle Ages, 400-1450, David Armstrong, Heinemann, 2002.

The Lewis Chessmen, James Robinson, The British Museum Press, 2004.

Mull, the Island and its Peoples, Jo Currie, Birlinn Ltd, 2001

Sea Room, Adam Nicolson, HarperCollins, 2001

Scottish Customs from the Cradle to the Grave, Margaret Bennett, Polygon, 1992

The Yellow on the Broom, Betsy Whyte, Futura Publications, 1986.

www.britishmuseum.org

Fantastic Books
Great Authors

Meet our authors and discover our exciting range:

- Gripping Thrillers
- Cosy Mysteries
- Romantic Chick-Lit
- Fascinating Historicals
- Exciting Fantasy
- Young Adult and Children's Adventures

Visit us at:
www.crookedcatpublishing.com

Join us on facebook:
www.facebook.com/crookedcatpublishing

Lightning Source UK Ltd.
Milton Keynes UK
UKOW03f2121210814

23735SUK00001B/8/P